JUST A NICE GIRL

The Complete

Cases of Shean Connell, Volume 1

1937–38

ROGER TORREY

illustrations by Arthur Rodman Bowker

cover by Harry Stoner

BLACK MASK

2025

Table of Contents

Hillbilly Stuff

This dick plays a tune with his .45

THE TRAIN STOPPED at Pinehurst as though stopping there was a new trick for it, and I got out of the rain and into a rickety station house. I set my bag down and went to the ticket window and asked:

"Anybody from Wilson's down here after me?"

The bird back of the wicket looked as if he hadn't been fed in months. Emaciated. He pointed at a big red-faced man who was pacing the floor, and said:

"That's Wilson! That's the so-and-such right there."

Only he used the right words.

I moved away from the window and over to Wilson and told him: "I'm Shean Connell. You're Wilson, aren't you?"

He said he was, and shook hands. I didn't like his looks one little bit but politeness didn't cost me anything and, after all, he was hiring me. He led me out to a car and said:

"I came after you myself, instead of sending my driver. It gives me a chance to tell you what's the matter."

"Matter enough," I said. "Beck, from my agency, came up here to act as your body-guard. He was killed and you still need a guard. I'm it. My agency's got the idea that the local law isn't making progress on the Beck killing. I've got the picture."

He led me out to a Ford station wagon. I shoved my bags in the back and we started off.

"I've been threatened," Wilson said.

"They told me that in my office."

By that time we were going down the road. He went on with:

"Two notes were sent me. Over—well, over two unfortunate accidents I've had. I remember what they said, though I've destroyed them. The first read: 'You got away with it twice now. That's enough.' The second read: 'The third time is your turn.' "

I said that was something and asked what the "Got away with it twice" stuff meant. What kind of accidents and what about them. He said:

"Well... on the first, the child's mother demanded an investigation. I was cleared, of course."

"What were you charged with?"

"Drunken driving. I was sober, of course."

"How old was the child?"

"About six, I understand."

"And the other thing? I can understand why the first stunt wouldn't make you popular."

"I happened to be hunting, with one of the local men as guide. Somehow, through clumsiness, he managed to shoot himself and died."

"Shot with your gun, I take it?"

"Well, yes. He was examining it and didn't understand it."

"And you figure a member of one of those two families is threatening you?"

He said that was it.

"You think that was why Beck was killed? Because he was protecting you from this trouble?"

"That seems evident."

It didn't seem evident to me. If somebody was out to kill Wilson from revenge, it seemed evident they'd just do the job. They wouldn't bother to write him letters about it first. And Beck had been killed in the village, Pinehurst, and that killing didn't add up with a revenge theory. None of it made sense.

About this time we pulled up in front of what looked like a hotel built of pine logs. That big. Two-storied and with windows set in funny angles in the sloping roof; a railed-in porch that circled the front and both sides. And the whole thing lit up like the Tower of Jewels at the 1915 San Francisco Exposition.

Wilson said, "Well, here we are. Of course, you want to remember we're in the woods and ten miles from the village. It's just a lodge, so you can't expect much in the line of comfort."

He led me inside then. The inside looked like what the well dressed lodge should wear. Fur rugs, mounted heads and guns hung on the walls, rough looking chairs and couches that looked as though they'd been made to order, and all the rest of that. The big room we went in had a fireplace that looked large enough to take a six foot log and Wilson told me proudly that this was just the length it would take.

And then I met Mrs. Wilson and the young Wilson kid.

Mrs. Wilson was little and faded and scared looking. Every time she spoke she looked at the Mister to see if she'd said the right thing. The kid was about twenty and as pretty as she could be, except for the times she looked at her father. Then she looked like one of the stuffed wildcats the old man had hanging around. As soon as I met them the old man said to me:

"Come along with me, Connell. I'll show you your room. Don't expect it to be much; we're really just camping out here."

The kid, whose name was Linda, looked at him as though she'd like to shoot him.

My room on the second floor was about twenty by twenty-four and was fitted up better than the apartment I'd left to go up in the wilds. Another fireplace, book cases on one side, six different kinds of liquor with glasses to match in a little built-in alcove, and an oversize bed. I didn't look but I wouldn't have been surprised if there'd been silk sheets on it.

"Of course, it isn't much," Wilson said.

I said, "You can let down your hair. We're alone at last."

"What d'ya mean, Connell?"

"You don't have to put on an act with me. I used to be in the music business and I've played piano for plenty of the fancy ladies."

He didn't like this and left me, after telling me lunch would be in twenty minutes. I stayed in the room for the twenty minutes; I had a notion I was going to see more of the big lug than I wanted and I couldn't see any use in following him around when I didn't have any reason for it.

LUNCH WAS ELABORATE. Too elaborate. After it, the three Wilsons and I tramped in the big front room where they had a Steinway concert grand. There was a sort of dull pause, everyone being too full of food to be bright, and Mrs. Wilson said, just to make conversation:

"I've heard Mr. Wilson speak of you so very many times, Mr. Connell."

She looked over at Wilson to see if she'd spoken out of turn. Wilson had told me he didn't want the family to know I was a detective, and he said in a hurry:

"Yes, Mr. Connell and I are old friends. I've known Mr. Connell for three years now."

I didn't like the stuffed shirt and decided to take him for a ride. I said, "Yeah! I was playing piano then. At the Dollar Club, out in Colma. I won't say it was the biggest clip joint I ever worked in, but it did wonderfully well considering its size."

Wilson got red in the face. The kid Wilson, Linda, came to life with a bang. She gave her papa a dirty look and said:

"Do you mean you used to play a piano at this place called the Dollar Club? And that you met Daddy there?"

"I don't remember where I met your father, Miss Wilson. But if he says it was three years ago when it happened, it happened at the Dollar Club."

Wilson was very red in the face and he was mopping at his forehead, even though the room wasn't too warm. Mrs. Wilson hadn't understood a word of what had been said and looked the part. The young Wilson, Linda, was grinning all over her face and you could see she was spinning the brain trying to figure some way to throw the harpoon at papa again.

I supposed I looked happy. I felt happy, anyway. Already it was a pleasure to see Wilson suffer. The young Wilson moved over to me and held out her hand. I didn't know what she wanted but she said:

"Come on."

I asked come on where and she told me she needed music. Piano music. The kind of music the Dollar Club patrons got.

She got it. "Aunt Hagar's Blues," "Beale Street Blues,"

"Entertainer's Rag," "Tiger Rag," and a bunch of stuff like that. She asked for "Tiger Rag" again and got it. She turned to her father again and asked:

"Do you remember Mr. Connell playing that at the Dollar Club, Dad?"

I quit on that one and went back to my seat on the couch. She followed me over and sat beside me and kept eying her dad all the time. Mrs. Wilson asked Wilson if he felt like playing Russian Bank and he did.

Anything to change the subject.

The kid said to me: "You don't play piano now, do you?"

I said I didn't.

"What do you do?"

"I'm a salesman. Hardware salesman."

"Don't fool me, Mr. Connell."

"I wouldn't, Miss Wilson."

"It's Linda, Mr. Connell."

"Well, then, it's Shean instead of Mr. Connell."

"And you're a detective."

"What makes you think that?"

She leaned over, across me, pretending to reach for a cigarette, and patted the bulge the gun made under my arm. She said, "I don't see why you men don't find another place to carry them. They show there every time."

"Not if you don't look for them."

She admitted there might be truth in this.

I wanted to go back to the village, but there was no hurry. I managed to get pretty well acquainted with the Wilson kid before I did.

Linda, to me.

ONE HOUR LATER, that afternoon, I dodged the Wilsons and headed back to the village. I'd known how big Pinehurst was before I'd left the city so I had the right clothes for the act I wanted to do. A new hat, not so new leather jacket, and a pair of trousers I'd bought on the lower end of Market. And new shoes. I didn't shave and the whiskers made it a perfect costume for a tin-horn gambler or a traveling road-house piano player who wasn't above playing in a parlor house if hungry.

The class of people you meet when you're dressed like that can tell you more about the local conditions and big shots than all the rest of the town added up. My aim was to find out all I could that might have a bearing on the mess Wilson thought he was in, and on Beck's killing.

First I went in a dirty-looking bar, down toward the end of the one main street, and when the bar man looked at me, I said:

"A shot!"

He poured a drink of just about the poorest whiskey I've ever tried to drink. By using will power I got it down without gagging. He looked me over and said:

"Stranger, huh?"

"Just got in. How're things?"

He waved his hand as though he was giving me the keys to the city. "Not good; not bad. There's quite a payroll up in the woods and the boys come to town over the weekends. Then they go back and earn more money."

I said, "Have one with me."

He did and I had one with him. I've always been curious about just what that whiskey he had was made from. Whiskey's supposed to be made from corn or rye but this wasn't; corn or rye couldn't be fixed up to taste that bad. He had a nickel in the slot phonograph lined along the wall beside four slot machines, and next to that a nickel piano, and after the three drinks and half an hour's talk I went over there and started to pound. Pound is the word. The thing hadn't been tuned since it had been moved in and some of the keys would stick so I'd have to lift them up. I managed to struggle through a couple of numbers and the bar man said, from where he'd been blowing his breath down the back of my neck:

"Say, guy, you're pretty good. I'm nuts about music."

I told him that's how I made a living. He winked at me, said, "You alone?"

"Sure!"

"Big May's looking for a girl."

"She got a piano?"

"Yeah! Last I heard she had a piano player though. I heard a couple of nights ago."

I went back to the bar and bought us both a drink and got confidential. I said, "Look! I'm a stranger, see. First time I made this route. I won't work a spot alone and I won't let my skirt work a spot alone. See! Is there any place in town where we could hook up?"

He grinned and looked wise. "I knew damn well you had a girl. You guys don't fool Danny. I never saw a piano player yet that wasn't a pimp."

I didn't laugh. The piano players he'd met had been working parlor houses or honky-tonks and I didn't doubt his word a bit. Right then a short husky duck with law written all over him came in and stood at the front of the bar and my pal went down to wait on him. I saw the husky one jerk a thumb toward me and my new pal, Danny, leaned over and whispered to him.

Then Danny got very busy at the back bar and the husky guy drifted down my way.

He looked good-natured. He said, "Going to stay in town, fella?"

"If I get a job."

"What kind of a job?"

"Well, I do restaurant work."

He laughed and grinned at me and showed me a gold eyetooth. He said, still with this grin: "You don't have to stall me. This town's open if you're right. Take your girl and go down to Greek Annie's and say I sent you. There's only two joints in town and you'll make more dough at Greek Annie's than you will at May's place. But listen! The town's open but we don't go for rough stuff. Get it?"

I said, "I catch."

THE WILSON FAMILY were out on the porch when I got back to the lodge late that afternoon.

Linda saw me first. She took a look at my clothes and giggled and said, "Going native on us Wilsons?"

Mrs. Wilson said, "My, Mr. Connell, I was beginning to worry about you. I thought you were lost, in the woods, you know."

Wilson just made a growling noise down in his throat.

I said, "I thought I'd walk around a bit. Pinehurst is a nice looking little town. I've met several people there I know. Old friends."

Linda looked at her papa and said, "That you made at the Dollar Club?"

Papa got red in the face. I went upstairs and changed my clothes and came back down and took a drink.

Linda and I got separated from the others, concerted effort I'll always think, and I said, "What have you got against your father, kid?"

She started looking like one of the stuffed wildcats inside. She said, "I hate him. He was at some awful place in Pinehurst and he got drunk. He ran over a little girl and lied out of it. He didn't even pay her hospital bill when she was in the hospital, or for the funeral when she died. Her people are very poor."

"I heard something about that."

"He isn't my father, anyway. He's my stepfather. I hate him."

I said I understood the latter from her manner and we joined the others. And then, after a while, Linda talked me into going inside and playing piano. I was glad enough to go; I figured I'd need practice for my night job.

And then we had dinner.

After dinner I begged off; said I had an appointment with a friend in Pinehurst. Linda followed me out on the porch and said:

"I don't know what you're planning, Shean, but the man before you was killed. Did you know that?"

I said I knew that. She said she couldn't understand why this happened. I told her it was a mystery to me, also, which wasn't the truth. I had a good idea. I piled in the coupé that Wilson let me use and she followed me over and leaned her elbows on the window.

"I've got to go," I said.

"Why don't you take me with you?"

I thought of my new piano playing job at Greek Annie's and

said I was sure she wouldn't like this friend I was to meet. She said she was sure she'd like all my friends.

With that I left for Greek Annie's.

IT TOOK THREE days to get the set-up right and I damn near wore out ten fingers in the three days. Greek Annie's was a port of call for every hustler, pimp, and no-good conniver in the country. Most of them were cheap tin-horns but there were three that looked like what I'd been expecting to find. Not high class crooks but smart enough to know what the score was at the sixth inning.

One was called Fats Mitchell. He used about five feet in height to carry about three hundred pounds. He had the biggest paunch I ever saw on a man that short and looked like a pear balanced on two matches. With the big end of the pear at the bottom. He spent his time at Annie's just pawing at the girls and giggling like a high school girl with hysterics.

The second was Tommy Pappas. A Greek. Short and dark and husky. He drank quite a bit and left the girls alone. He didn't have any credit coming to him for this last; none of the girls would have a thing to do with him.

The third one was just called Harold. A man about forty-five. He wore glasses, which probably caused the Harold nickname. He claimed to be a Russian, and his favorite argument when drunk was that the part of Russia he came from was where the Caucasian race really originated. He might have been right; I didn't argue it. He was tall, rather thin, and gray. Gray hair, light slaty gray eyes, and the same sort of skin. Gray clothes, even. He seemed to me to be the toughest baby of the bunch.

These three stuck around together most of the time. Fats

Mitchell owned a pool and gambling room, and the other two dealt cards for him. After they'd close the pool room, they'd drop down to Annie's and I'd get a chance to look them over. I couldn't tell whether Fats packed a gun or not, because his clothes fitted him like a burlap sack around a pig, but he could well have. I picked the Greek for a knife and I could see the bulge a gun made under Harold's left arm.

Nice people, all three of them. They didn't pay any attention to me, and I was glad of it. All I was classed as was a traveling piano player and they wouldn't pick anybody like that for a friend of Wilson.

They were just the kind to work the frame I thought was coming to a head; I had to figure some kind of an extortion angle, the way things were lined up, and these three were that type. The threatening letters didn't fit with a revenge theory, regardless of what Wilson thought.

THE FOURTH MORNING Wilson woke me. He came in, looking as though he'd sell out cheap, and said:

"I've got another letter."

"Let me tell you what's in it," I said. "It tells you that your time is up but that you can maybe buy yourself out for a little dough. That is, what would be a little dough for you. Is that it?"

He said that was it. He handed me a note that said he could live in peace for only twenty-thousand dollars, and that he was to get this money ready to hand over. He was to keep this money handy and he'd be told what to do with it.

I said, "You going to pay it?"

"What's money compared to a human life?"

I didn't answer this but let him think it over. He wasn't slow.

In a moment he said, "How did you know this would be a demand for money?"

"You hired me as a detective, didn't you?"

"Do you know who sent me this?"

"I've got an idea but I can't prove it. I've got an idea who killed Beck, from my agency, the man before me, but I can't prove that either. That's what I really want to know. He was a good friend and they never gave him a chance. He got four slugs in him, just a little distance from one of the village joints, and I want to know who did it."

He started to walk up and down the room and said that common sense told him it must be some member of the two families who'd been concerned in the unfortunate accidents; that these families had already made trouble for him and that undoubtedly either one or both were behind this dastardly blackmailing attempt and Beck's killing. He didn't stop to think that a revenge killer isn't after money.

I said, "Attempt! You just the same as told me you were going to pay it."

"But, Connell! A man could hide among the trees with a rifle and pick me off when I stepped out on the porch."

"Sure. They could dynamite the house if they wanted to. They could sneak in the kitchen and put poison in the soup. For that matter, they could start a little mob scene in the village and get the villagers up here to lynch you. I'm sorry to say it but you're not too popular in the village."

"I know it." He groaned this. "That's why I'm selling this place. I've got to get away."

"When are you selling?"

"At once. The first of next week."

"Anybody in the village know that?"

He looked at me as though this question didn't make sense and I said, "Speak up, man! It's important."

"I discussed the affair with the local banker. He's taking this place off my hands."

I said, "Let me figure it over a bit. I'll talk it over with you later."

I didn't need any time to think it over; I'd done that before. What I had to do was figure some way to break it before the first of the next week. Monday and the pay-off would arrive together. Whoever was after him would get action before he sold out and left. News like that sale would travel.

GREEK ANNIE WASN'T a Greek but she was dark enough to be one. I went to work early that day and got there before there was any business. Two of the gals were downtown some place, another was washing her socks and so on in the bathroom, leaving the door open so she could join in the talk. The fourth and last gal was out in the kitchen trying to talk the Chink cook into putting lettuce on a chicken sandwich she was also trying to get him to make for her. Charley, the cook, was objecting loudly and brokenly to this idea.

Greek Annie said to me, "I've been watching you, Professor. What's the racket?"

They always call the pianist "Professor" in a spot like that. I looked as innocent as I could and stalled.

"What d'ya mean, what's the racket?"

The girl in the bathroom called out, "Hey, Annie, you're getting thick. He's sizing up the spot and trying to figure if that tramp of his could make any dough working against me."

Annie said to the girl, "Take care of your laundry and shut up," and to me: "What's the racket?"

"No racket. Town got hot for me so I moved. That's all."

Annie leaned over close to me and lowered her voice. "I notice you pay more attention to what's going on than you do to the ivories."

"It gets monotonous, Annie, this playing all night when other people are partying. You know how it is."

"If it's that."

"Sure it's that."

The girl from the kitchen out-talked the Chink. She came in, bearing a sandwich three inches thick, came over to me and said:

"Listen! D'ya know one I like? It's an old-timer. 'Do You Ever Think of Me?'"

I said I knew it. She said, "Why don't you play it?"

"Nuts! It's too early to start working."

She swaggered over to the door, which was open, and started looking out. Annie said, as though she didn't mean anything by it:

"D'ya know, Professor, just before you started to work they found a stiff just down the road from this spot here."

I swung around and played four bars of "Frankie and Johnny."

"You're wrong," she said. "He didn't belong to any of my girls. Peggy here, has got a man. You met him. Billie and Grace have. Shirley's an outlaw."

Shirley was the girl in the bathroom and Annie calling her an outlaw meant that Shirley had no consort. Shirley stuck her head from the bathroom door, laughed and said:

"And Shirley's going to stay an outlaw. All a man does is keep you poor."

I said, "What was the guy knocked off for? There must have been a reason."

Annie said, "I make it a point to mind my own business and nobody else's. So I don't know. But I happen to know this stiff worked for old man Wilson, up at the lodge."

Peggy swung around from the door with most of the sandwich gone. She said, "Yeah! Old Sugar Wilson. The last time he come over here he dropped over a hundred bucks."

Then Shirley came out lugging a bunch of socks and a bunch of pink silk. She said, "We heard the shots. Fats Mitchell and that damned Greek pal of his was here. And Harold."

Peggy said: "No they weren't. They'd left just before that. The guy was here first, don't you remember? He spent a little dough and asked a lot of questions. Then Fats and Harold and the Greek came in and he talked to them and bought another couple of rounds. Then Fats and the Greek and Harold left and then the guy left. Then we heard the shots. I remember it all."

I looked away from Peggy and saw Annie looking at me. Her eyes were squinted a little and she looked as though she was trying to figure what I thought about it.

I said, "I heard about the guy getting killed but I didn't know it happened that close to here. It's a good thing I wasn't working here then."

Shirley said, "Why?"

"Well, you know. The cops and all. I'd have had to answer a bunch of questions about where I came from and all that. I got a break that it happened before I got here."

Shirley said, "I get the point!" and went out in the kitchen to hang up her wash. Peggy followed her. Then Greek Annie leaned over to me again and said, under her breath:

"Like I say, I mind my own business. I'd hate to have my piano player get the same dose because of nose trouble."

I said, "I don't get it."

"It came out, when they checked this guy over, that he was from some detective agency in the city. I heard that. I just thought the same agency might still be on the job. Understand me, I haven't said anything."

I told her again that I didn't understand.

"You don't understand then," she said. "I just happened to see you talking to that Wilson kid, Linda, or whatever her name is. This afternoon up by the post-office. D'ya get what I mean now?"

I said, "I get it."

She was just telling me she knew I was a cop.

I SPENT THE rest of the evening adding things up. Beck, from my agency, the Apex, must have had the same idea I had about an extortion racket being pulled on Wilson. He must have said something to show this. He could have been killed by any of the three men I'd picked as rough enough to do the job. They had the opportunity.

And with Greek Annie having me spotted as an agency cop, this wasn't so good.

I didn't think she'd do any talking, that is, on purpose. But she drank with the customers hour in and hour out and she might let something slip. If she said anything to any of the girls that worked for her, the thing might as well be published in the paper. The girl would tell her man and he'd spread the news.

It went along like this until a little after eleven. There were three of the girls and five men in the front room, one couple dancing. Then the bell rang, one long and three short buzzes.

Greek Annie said, "It's law. It's O.K.," and went to the door, and the same cop I'd met in the bar when I first got to town came in. He came over to me, very businesslike, and said:

"Connell, I want you. Come along."

Annie said, "What's the beef?"

The cop said, "You keep out of this, Annie. It's no skin off your neck and it's liable to be if you butt in."

Annie put both hands on her hips and squared off. She said: "Listen, Fritz! Don't come in my place and take that tone with me. I won't have it, do you understand? I want to know what's the rap against Connell and I want to know it now. I want to know how much bail money to bring down for him. He's working for me and I stay with my people."

She sounded as though she was a school-teacher talking to a sulky five-year-old. Fritz looked the five-year-old part. He hung his head, said:

"We want to ask him a few questions, is all, Annie. It ain't a pinch."

"If Connell isn't back here in an hour I'm going down to the station after him. That plain?"

Fritz said this was plain and I got my hat and followed him out. He led me down the road a bit, said:

"It's no pinch, Connell! I didn't want to crack it in the spot, in front of people, but old man Wilson wants you. Somebody took a crack at him, up at the lodge. He was sitting in front of a window and somebody shot at him."

"Hit him?"

"Hell, no." He sounded as if this was bad news. "Lousy shooting. They busted a floor lamp about a foot to the right of his head. He's so damn scared he can't hardly talk."

"How'd you know where to find me?"

"Miss Wilson phoned in and asked us to locate you. I was on the desk and asked her to describe you. She said how you were dressed and that you played piano and I remembered you got this job with Annie."

Small town police went up a grade right then as far as I was concerned. I said, "Nice remembering, guy."

By this time we were where I'd left the coupé I was using. I climbed in and the cop leaned on the door and asked, "You working on that Apex man being killed?"

I said that this tied in. He said then, very earnestly: "Get the picture. There's less than three thousand people live here. Four policemen. And one Mayor and five councilmen. The Mayor owns the house Greek Annie rents. One of the councilmen owns Big May's place. Fats Mitchell's sister is married to the Mayor's brother. It's like that. We just work for wages, if you know what I mean."

I said, "I catch. Think nothing of it."

I started the motor and he told me something else. He leaned in close and said, "And Greek Annie's my second cousin, though neither she or I are proud of it."

I said: "I get it!" again, and started toward Wilson's Lodge. The cousin business explained away the scolding Annie had given him. And after the way he'd talked about the Mayor's tie-up with Fats Mitchell I didn't think he'd do any talking about the reason I was in town. I rather liked this Fritz.

WILSON'S LODGE WAS having company. The town's only police car was parked in front of it along with another that looked as though it might be from the sheriff's office. And a white California State Trooper's car to keep them company. I drove my coupé around to the back, got in through the kitchen, and sent the Filipino I found there to tell Miss Linda I wanted to see her by herself.

She came back as though she'd been expecting me. She said, "Where've you been? I've had the police looking for you."

I said, "They found me. How's the pop?"

"Scared stiff."

"What cops are in there?"

"The Chief of Police and another policeman, a Deputy Sheriff, and a State man."

"Pop's got protection, then."

She giggled. "He doesn't feel safe even with all that. He's trying to talk the Chief into arresting the families of the two people he killed and the Chief won't. The Chief hadn't better; those people have friends in town and if those friends found that Dad got those people thrown in jail they'd come out here and lynch Dad. Probably the Chief, too."

"I don't want this law to see me. I know all the law I want to know already."

"Dad's told them all about you. You might as well go on in."

I said, "That damn fool!" and minded her. She followed me. I think she thought I was going to bawl out her old man.

The Chief of Police looked like an ex-bartender and I found out afterwards this was what he'd been. A nice old fellow, though, and out in deep water over his head. The other cop was just a kid and he spent his time staring at the floor and shuffling his feet. The lodge furnishings had him dazed. The Deputy Sheriff was a lean dark man who was chewing tobacco. He looked as if he'd know his way around in the woods but that this was out of his line. The State man just stood over at the side and watched what was going on. From the way he acted he wasn't much interested and I didn't blame him.

Wilson had the floor and was walking up and down it. He'd stop and shake his fist at the poor old Chief and bellow out:

"This is an outrage. I want those people under lock and key."

The Chief would tell Wilson again that he, the Chief, couldn't very well do that. No one had any evidence against them. Then Wilson would demand the same action from the Deputy Sheriff and the State man and get the same answer. He was getting no place fast. I came in and he swung on me and almost shouted:

"And you! Here I was almost murdered and where are you? What am I paying you for? Hey? Answer me."

I said, "If I do, you'll wish I hadn't. What in hell's the matter with you? You aren't hurt, are you? Don't try that Almighty stuff on me or I'll slap the words back down your throat."

He stopped walking as though he'd run into something solid. He opened his mouth and goggled at me. I didn't give him time to get set but went on with:

"You're acting the damn fool all over the place. What in hell's the matter with you? If you make charges against those people and don't prove them, they'll sue you for more money than there is in the mint. And if you shoot off your mouth to the police the way you're doing you'll get just what little cooperation they're forced to give you. These men are here trying to help you; give them a chance."

He closed his mouth, then opened it again. I looked over at the State cop and saw him hold his hands together above his head and shake them to show his applause. He had a little stiff black mustache and there were a lot of teeth showing under this from his grin.

Wilson still hadn't gotten his breath and I figured that last blast of mine made a good exit line.

I took it. And Linda with me.

We waited on the porch for the pride and power of the police. Linda said, "I don't like my step-dad, I hate him, but it's a sneaking trick. Shooting at him through a window like that."

"Nobody was trying to hit him, Linda. If anybody wanted to hit him, he'd have been a cinch. This was just to scare him into getting the money ready."

I'd told her about the note he'd gotten. We'd reached the confidential stage some time before that; all she didn't know was where I was playing piano.

She said, "But Dad got this money late this afternoon. I drove him down."

I said that was different, and then the law came out and this gave me the chance to pass on the information I knew someone was waiting for.

I stopped them all. I said, "I didn't want to say anything in front of old Mr. Flannel Mouth in there, but here's the score. The old fool got twenty grand in cash today and somebody's trying to scare him loose from it. Get the picture?"

The old Chief, the Deputy Sheriff, and the State man said they got it. The dopy looking policeman just stood there with his mouth open and looked as though he didn't know whether it was snowing or Sunday.

The Chief said that no one should keep that much money with no protection; and that maybe he should spend the night there as a guard. I said that being a guard was what I was hired for and that he shouldn't bother himself. I made it very plain that the money was in the house and that there was no safe. I even said, "Wilson sleeps by the front of the house and I've got a room at the other end. When he goes to bed I'll see that he and his money are locked in."

They straggled toward their cars then and I followed the State man to his. He looked the quickest on the up-take.

I said, "Do me a favor. When you get to town, look up a cop called Fritz. He's on nights; will probably be at the station. Tell him I asked him to find out whether Fats Mitchell, Tommy Pappas, and a guy called Harold were around town at the time Wilson was shot at. Get it? Tell him to keep it hush-hush."

The State man showed me the white teeth again. He said, "I got it. A tip, huh! Anything solid on those three yet?"

I said, "No! But I'm willing to bet one of them is the one that popped off Beck, from my agency, last week. And if Wilson don't get in the way, I'm willing to bet I prove it."

"Wilson's a pest, huh?"

"He's the other part of the horse." He pulled out and I went back to Linda, and we stayed out on the porch for a while. Wilson stayed in the house with the blinds drawn.

EVERYBODY WAS IN bed by twelve o'clock. All but me. I was sitting by my door and I'd left it wide open. My room was dark and the hall was almost that way; just a little light coming up from the stairwell from a night lamp left burning at the foot. The chair was comfortable and I hadn't been getting too much sleep, and I was dozing a bit by three o'clock. But the window at the end of the hall made a little noise when it slid up and this snapped me out of it.

Whoever it was had to go right by my door to get to Wilson's room, so I just waited. I pulled the hammer of my gun back, pulling back the trigger at the same time so there'd be no betraying click at half and full cock. I got out of my chair and stood by the side of the door.

There were two of them. They came by me on tiptoe, going toward Wilson's room at the end of the hall, and I let them alone until they got there. They tried the door and found it locked, then squatted down by the door and tinkered with the lock.

Then I stepped out in the hall and said, "That's enough! Hold it!"

The stairs were between us and maybe ten feet from them. I was twenty, maybe twenty-five from the stairs. Both of them had been sitting on their heels and they stood when they saw me. There wasn't enough light for me to see their faces but enough for me to see light flash from a gun one of them held. He brought it up and shot and I fired back.

The fellow with the gun was on the inside, away from the stairs. The other made a plunging dive for them but I hadn't time to stop him; the bird with the gun was getting ready to try for me again. I shot just before he did and he slammed back against Wilson's door, but he still had enough left in him to raise his gun again.

There was no help for it. I shot him again and as near center as I could. There wasn't enough light in the hall to really aim, but I was used to my gun and was willing to bet I hadn't missed his belt buckle two inches either way.

This time he went down. The hall was narrow and low ceil-inged, and my gun was a .45. My three shots and his one had made plenty of noise and now we had echoes to help. I could hear Mrs. Wilson and Linda screaming even through this din, and I could hear Wilson bellowing:

"Connell! Help! Help!"

I didn't help Wilson and I didn't stop to look at the man I'd shot. I went down the stairs, three at a time, after the one who'd got away. I got to the foot of the stairs just as the front door was slamming and I got out on the porch in time to see him half-way between the lodge and where the woods started.

He was about a hundred feet away, maybe a little more. He was running, all bent over, but I had bright moonlight to help my side. I settled down and shot once, and found that the excitement and the run down the stairs had made me plenty shaky.

He didn't stop with the shot. It just speeded him up, though I hadn't thought this would be possible. On the second one I thought I'd got him. He stumbled but then he caught himself. He was on the edge of the woods when I let the third and last one go at him and I knew I'd missed when I shot.

There was no use following him. From the way he was running he could make three feet to my two and that was giving him none the best of the bet. I went back in the house and up the stairs and found the family in the hall.

Wilson and Linda were by the man I'd shot. Mrs. Wilson was leaning her head out of her door and she showed more life than any time since I'd met her. She saw me come up the stairs and she asked, "What happened, Mr. Connell?"

"I said, "Attempted robbery, Mrs. Wilson.""

"Is that man dead?"

"I think so."

"Is it one of the—a member of the families who've been sending my husband threatening letters?"

"I don't know."

I was standing by her then and we were well away from everybody else, though Wilson was bawling for me to join him. Mrs. Wilson almost whispered, "I hope it isn't. Those poor people have had trouble enough."

I said that was right and went to the man I'd shot. And got a surprise. I'd have been willing to bet it was either Tommy Pappas or Harold but it was a cheap punk kid I'd seen hanging around Fats Mitchell's card room. There he was, deader than last week's news.

There was a little nick in his right ear that had come from my first shot. There was a slug through his left shoulder from my second. And I'd centered his belt buckle; it was smashed out of shape and torn at one edge where the third slug had passed through it.

Linda looked more than a little sick. She said to me, "Oh, Shean! I didn't know it would be so terrible."

I didn't feel too well myself. I'd thought I was baiting a trap for Fats Mitchell, Tommy Pappas, and Harold, and all I'd done was get a cheap two-bit hustler. He still had his gun in his hand.

I said to Wilson, "Just throw something over him and don't move him. That gun, with an exploded shell, will prove it was self defense."

"You didn't mean to do it, did you, Shean?" Linda asked.

I said that there was no way to avoid it; that the man had shot at me and intended to keep on shooting. Wilson looked puzzled and said:

"I've never seen this man before in my life."

I didn't answer this but went downstairs and telephoned the police station and the Sheriff's office. There was no more sleep for anybody after that.

WE HAD COMPANY for breakfast at ten o'clock the next morning and I had an appetite, though maybe I shouldn't have had. The Chief of Police, the Deputy Sheriff, and the same State man. They left right after that, though not until the State man had taken me to the side and said:

"This is a tough break for you, Connell. You're spotted as a agency dick now and you'll have hell getting any dope on that Beck killing."

"I'm hired to keep Wilson safe. I've got ideas on that killing. I think I've got a line on who's back of this; it's straight extortion I think."

He grinned and asked me whether I'd rather find who'd killed Beck, my colleague, or see Wilson in his grave. He didn't expect an answer and didn't get one.

After they'd left, Linda and I sat out on the porch and she said:

"Dad's going to sell this place next week and we're moving to the city. Will I see you then, Shean?"

"Constantly, I hope."

"I like it here."

"If your Dad gets over his scare he may not sell."

"If! He's so scared now he's hysterical."

She was telling the truth. Old man Wilson really had the jitters. He was smart and that made it worse; he had enough imagination to really do a nice job of worrying.

Fritz, the policeman, maybe had some information for me and I wanted to wander around a bit. I knew Greek Annie would have heard about the row, as well as everybody else in town, and knew that my piano playing days for her were over. But still I wanted to see her. So I said to Linda:

"I've got to go to town. I'll be back in two or three hours, I think."

"Take me with you."

There was no reason why I shouldn't, as long as I parked her somewhere when I went to Greek's Annie's place.

I said, "I will, if you can keep busy for about an hour by yourself. I've got an errand to do that I can't take you with me on."

She said that was fine with her but we didn't leave until around one o'clock. And then only after an argument; Wilson didn't want to be left by himself.

There was one fairly nice bar in the town, even though it was small. We went in a booth and I bought Linda a drink and told her: "Now you wait here for me. I'll be back as soon as I can."

"You'll be careful?"

I said I'd try to be. I stood up and started to leave, but she caught me by the sleeve and said:

"Look! Look, Shean!"

All there was to see was a tall dark man with a scarred cheek. A man of about forty. He was heading for the back, toward the men's room, and I said:

"What about him?"

"That's Angelo Pacelli. The father of the little girl Dad ran over. He's got five others, and the littlest one is the cutest baby you ever saw in your life. I see them every now and then."

She saw them when she took down groceries and money, but I didn't tell her I knew about that. Pacelli came back, saw Linda and came over. He held his hat in his hands and told her his wife and the kids were fine and that he was glad to see her. He acted as if this last was the truth.

When I left he was telling her what Pietro had said when Mama Pacelli had spanked him for playing hookey from school.

Annie and all four girls were at the spot. Even Charley, the cook. They all flocked around me, in the parlor, and Annie said:

"I knew you had an angle. You played too much piano for a road-house bum."

Shirley said, "I didn't pick you as a copper, though." She sounded hurt.

I said, "Well, I'll tell you. I'm an agency cop and that isn't the same as a regular cop. A man from my agency got killed and that makes it sort of personal. It was a dirty trick to play on you girls, getting a job here and all that, but I had to do it."

Shirley mourned, "A cop! My Gawd! You'd think I could pick a cop; I've been in enough trouble with them."

Annie took me in another room. She said, "You're smart enough to get the local set-up. It was good riddance, your getting rid of that punk last night. But your working for Wilson puts you behind the eight ball. I'm telling you that when he left here the day he ran over that little Italian girl he was so drunk he couldn't hit the floor with his hat two times out of three. That's just for you, mind you. That's not for a jury; I'm not mixing up in any trials. Anything you learned here, you found out about some place else."

"Don't be a fool, Annie. I wouldn't spill. I'm a agency cop but I still have friends."

She lowered her voice. "And if I was you, I wouldn't turn my back on either Fats Mitchell or Harold or that damn Greek Pappas."

I said: "I understand."

They all followed me to the door and shook hands with me and said that they'd miss me. Shirley even went a step past that. She held my hand longer than was necessary and said:

"Well, good-by. Even if you are a cop, I like you. If you ever start making an honest living, look me up, Annie here will tell you where I am. I'll keep in touch with her."

"I doubt if I'll quit, kid."

"You and I could make a lot of dough up around that dam they're building in Washington. It's wide open, they tell me."

I said I'd think it over and left, with them waving good-by at me. Nice people. Even if not moral. And Annie had the same idea about Fats and Harold and Pappas that I had. It was worth knowing.

Fritz was in the same bar I'd first met him. I went in and the bar man scowled at me and slid me my whiskey as though it hurt him to do it. We'd been pals up to then. Fritz moved down the bar to me and said, from the side of his mouth:

"None of them three were around in sight at the time Wilson was shot. Fats, Harold, and the Greek were all missing from the scene."

"Did that kid cop that was with the Chief last night crack about the money Wilson had?"

"He did until I shut him up."

"That mouth of his got that punk burglar killed last night. I wasn't aiming for him."

"Fats and the Greek and Harold were around when the talk was going around about Wilson having all that dough cached there. I was in Fats' place at the time. I saw all three there. Fats and Harold come in together some time before that. The Greek came in alone, later."

This backed up my idea about one of the three being the one that I'd shot at when he'd run from Wilson's.

The barman came down then and leaned over to me and said, "Get that drink down you and get out. I run a clean place and I don't want any stoolies hanging around here."

This was out of a clear sky. He was so mad he was shaking all over and he had a beer bottle gripped by the neck.

Fritz said, "You take it easy, Danny."

"He's working for Wilson, ain't he? I'll have no friend of that baby killing —— in my place. Get him to hell out of here before I let go."

Fritz said to me, "Come on; we'll leave."

We got outside and he said, "Old Danny is a good guy, but he's got a mean temper. He thinks about things for a while and then gets mad all in a bunch. He hates Wilson because Wilson ran over that little Wop kid and then dogged it."

"Wilson isn't popular, is he?"

"If he died," Fritz sounded very solemn, "everybody in town would turn out for the funeral."

I said I understood how the town felt.

LINDA WAS STILL waiting and none too pleased about my being away for so long. We went out on the street and to the car, and the State trooper who'd been at the lodge came up. He said, "Hello, Miss Wilson," and to me: "Could I speak to you a minute, Connell? There's quite a lot of talk going around town about you. I keep out of the local troubles as much as I can and probably hear things the local police don't on that account. D'ya know what I mean?"

"What's the talk?"

"The story is that you blasted down that guy in the hall last night without giving him a chance. He was a local boy, except for the time he spent away in reform schools and State prisons, and his friends seem to think you ought to ride a rail out of town. You and Wilson both."

I said, "I'm beginning to think that would be the right way for Wilson to travel when he goes places but why in hell should they pick on me? I just work here. All I did last night was shoot back at a man that was shooting at me. Who did this guy I killed last night run around with?"

"He hung around Fats Mitchell's place. That's all I know about him."

I thanked the State man and got in the car with Linda. The State man followed me over and I said, "You stationed here all the time?"

"I'm supposed to patrol between here and Regas. I'm sticking around until this breaks, though."

Linda said, "Thank you, officer."

She was driving. We went out of town, going along slowly, and into the woods road that led to the lodge. She was loafing along at twenty miles an hour and talking about the things we'd do and see when we were both in the city, and about then we hit a stretch of road that ran straight for maybe a quarter of a mile. She opened the car up a little bit and right then the windshield starred in the middle, between us, and I heard a noise that sounded like a whip crack in my ear.

Linda said, "Wha—" There was that much lapse of time before we heard the rifle. I reached over and jerked the wheel toward me, hard, and the coupé left the road and went through a little ditch and smashed into a tree. I'd pulled Linda from under the wheel just before we crashed, so she wouldn't be hurt from being slammed into the wheel. I got the car door open with my other hand and yanked her out, then dragged her over behind a fallen log.

She said, "What in the world? Was somebody shooting at us?"

"Not at us. At me. But they might hit you."

She gasped at this but it didn't scare her. Her voice was steady enough when she said, "What are we going to do?"

"Are you too shaky to walk? The car's wrecked."

"Of course not."

"Then we're going to walk back to town. It's nearer than the lodge. Somebody's getting worried, which is fine."

"But Shean! Won't they follow us?"

"The kind of guy that hides in the brush for his Sunday shot won't take that chance."

I tried to make this sound good but I doubt if it did. Whoever it was, had a rifle and we were cold meat if he wanted to crowd us. All he had to do was get one decent sight and we were gone. I wanted to keep Linda out of it so I said:

"Now you go first. Keep in the woods until you get around the bend, then get out in the road and run like hell. I'll follow you."

She got the idea. She stuck out her lower lip and said, "I won't. I'm going to stay with you."

I didn't argue but said, "Let's go." By the time I'd talked her into going by herself the gunman would have time to sneak up on us and she'd be in as much danger as she'd been in when in the car. Anybody dirty enough to work an Indian ambush on us that way was dirty enough to kill the girl to keep her mouth shut. A bird like that wouldn't take any chances of her having seen him and being able to identify him.

There was fairly thick brush until we got around the bend in the road and then we really put on speed. We got to town, out of breath, and I kept on going until I saw the State man.

I told him what had happened and he said, "I'll drive you out. The car wrecked bad?"

"It'll have to be towed in."

"Anything of yours in it?"

"No."

He thought a moment, said, "You go out to the lodge in a taxi. The Chief has got what passes for a finger-printing outfit in his office. Somebody took a correspondence school course. I'll borrow the outfit from him and go out and look over that car, then have it towed in here."

Linda said, "But the man shot at us from the woods. He wasn't in the car."

"He might have looked the car over." The State man, whose name was Kendricks, smiled at her as though she'd slipped. "Whoever sees the car there will stop and look it over to make sure nobody's hurt. If I can get there before a lot of other people make prints all over it, I might get that shooter's."

NEITHER LINDA NOR I told Wilson anything about the Indian act somebody worked on us. He was just about frantic with fear already and this news wouldn't have helped him a bit. Linda told him she'd blown a front tire and smacked the coupé against a tree and that was that. He was in such bad shape I didn't want her to give him the mail, because I had a notion what was in it. But she said he had to get the bad news sooner or later and that it might as well be then.

The letter was in a dirty, cheap looking envelope. Both the envelope and the sheet of paper inside were printed, as the former notes had been, with a pencil. The printing itself was badly formed, so awkwardly that I decided it had been written that way on purpose. The note read:

You've got the money yet. At five this afternoon start walking down the road toward town. You will be stopped. Be alone and you won't be hurt.

It was after four then. Wilson, his hand shaking so he almost dropped the note, looked at his watch and found this out. He stammered at me: "What should I do?"

I said, "I'd take the money and the walk. I'd rather be a live coward than a dead hero. And if I told you not to go, you'd go anyway and you know you would."

"I don't understand that remark, Mr. Connell."

"Oh nuts! You'd stand on your head on the porch until five, then get down on your hands and knees and push a peanut with your nose down that road if the note told you to do it. You're scared stiff and both you and I know it."

He didn't deny it but looked as though he was ready to shake apart. He was almost crying when he said, "They'll maybe kill me."

I said, "They're fools if they do. They've got a good thing in you, if you're careful. They'll take every dime you've got, if they can keep you alive and able to get money from banks."

"You think they won't hurt me?"

I said I didn't think they would.

The main road that led to Pinehurst from the lodge went right by the front of the house. I knew that if I cut through the woods for a couple of miles that I'd hit a back road that also led to Pinehurst. And I knew unless I was lucky and picked a ride, I'd have a five-mile walk into town on this. I told Wilson to start out at five, with his money, and that I'd try to get it back for him.

I told him all he had to do was just what whoever stopped him told him to do and fixed it for Linda to start at six in the big car to pick him up. He'd have been stopped by then. She was to watch along the side of the road, just in case he'd been left tied, but she had strict orders to bring him into town.

Then I wandered out to the garage in back of the lodge, and ducked into the timber with as little fuss as I could, just on the chance somebody was watching the house for anything suspicious. I had to take a chance on getting to town on time over that back road; I didn't think the extortioners would hurt Wilson, but I knew they'd be a lot more liable to hurt him if I went down the main road a few minutes ahead of him.

I found the back road in about half an hour and fifteen minutes later found the first break I'd had since I'd come to Pinehurst. An old Model-T Ford, with a big-boned husky changing a tire on it. He was going great guns on a hand pump when I got there.

I said, "Let me spell you, chief."

He said, "Goddlemighty yes!"

The two of us got air in that tire in less than five minutes. And then the two of us went careening through the trees just miles an hour. This big bird turned the car loose and wide open and, as near as I could see, just let it find it's own way along the road. At least he spent the five minutes it took us to get into town turned around in his seat so he could face me and ask me questions.

I was so nervous I might even have told him the truth. But he got us into town at five-twenty.

Kendricks, the State trooper, was leaning against the front of the town's one bank. He looked startled when he saw me climb from the Ford, and started toward me. I said, "Thank you!" to the Model-T man and he said:

"Don't mention it, Mister," and jazzed the Ford off down the street as though it was a piece of tin gone crazy.

Kendricks came up and said, "How come you tied up with Wild Bill? Every time he comes to town I give him a tag for reckless driving and he pays 'em and says it's worth it to see the town folks duck for shelter."

I said, "You seen Fats Mitchell and those two hoodlums of his?"

"Fats and Harold went driving out the lodge road. The Greek, Tommy Pappas, is keeping an eye on Fats' place for him. I saw him just a bit ago."

I said, "Want to come along?"

He looked at me and brightened up and said, "I wouldn't miss it."

FATS MITCHELL'S PLACE was long and dark and

dirty. There was a lunch counter on one side, God help the man that ate there, and this faced a bar that really did business. There were three pool tables then, and the back of the place was full of card tables. Each was set by itself, and there were brass chains around each table to keep kibitsers from breathing on the back of the players' necks. Two of the tables were busy—a panguingi game going at one and a hokey game at the other.

Tommy Pappas was playing hokey, which is four card stud poker. One card down and three cards up. When I got there he was peeking at his hole card palmed in his right hand. He put it back on the table, and awkwardly used his right hand again to toss in a chip.

The dealer was bald and very big. His nose was flattened against his face and looked as though there was no bone in it. He wheezed through this: "Tommy's in. Who else?"

A couple more put in their antes and the flat-nosed man tossed out cards. Pappas got an ace and threw out a blue chip. Again with his right hand. He looked up and saw Kendricks and me standing there and said:

"Hello, Kendricks."

He didn't speak to me but the look he gave me was almost audible. His eyes were as flat and cold and hard looking as a snake's. I just got that one quick look and then he went back to staring at cards. He carried his left arm stiff and as though it bothered him.

Finally the deal got through, with Pappas winning the pot. He grinned, showing stained, dirty looking teeth, and said, "Hah! Two aces," and raked in the money with his right hand.

I said, "Pappas! What's the matter with your left arm?"

He'd been expecting it and was set for it. His right hand

snaked up over his shoulder and to the back of his neck, and when he brought it ahead I ducked down on my heels. The knife made a streak of light when it went over me, and it kept going until it hit a rack of pool balls and clattered to the floor.

Kendricks said, "Pappas!"

Pappas went for the gun that was in the drawer in front of the dealer. He shoved the flat-nosed man, who didn't know what it was all about, in the chest and the flat-nosed man went tipping back, chair and all. The five men at the table got away fast.

Pappas jerked the drawer open while he was half-turned from me, then brought the gun up and in sight and faced me. I could see his legs in the shadow of the table and I was waiting for that gun to come in sight.

I shot him in the right kneecap and that .45 slug took his leg from under him and spun him like a pin wheel. He fell side-wise, and as he fell he threw the gun he held high in the air.

Kendricks was on him in that second. Kendricks didn't know Pappas' knee had been shot from under him and he tried to lift him up by the handcuffs he'd put on him, but Pappas was only half-way up when he fainted.

I said to Kendricks, "You'll have to carry him. I've busted his leg."

One of the innocent bystanders tried to hand me the gun Pappas had thrown away and I said, "Give it to the policeman."

Kendricks pocketed it. Then the broken-nosed man untangled himself from his chair, got up and said, "Did he get away?"

Kendricks said, "What in hell you talking about?"

"Ain't it a hold-up?"

Kendricks said it was no hold-up, just a pinch, and sent one of the bystanders to call the town ambulance. The guy started away and I said, "Tell it to come to the back."

Kendricks looked at me and I stalled with: "It's closer. Not so far to carry him." I didn't want Fats and Harold to see an ambulance in front, just in case they came back early.

Fritz, the town copper I knew, came busting through the crowd then and Kendricks turned Pappas over to him.

Kendricks said, "Get him to the hospital and see he stays there. He will; he's in no shape to walk. And tell the doctor I want to know how long ago it was he got the bullet in his left arm."

Then he turned at me and said, "That's what you were getting at, wasn't it, Connell?"

I said, "You got it."

Fritz was back by the time Kendricks had the crowd cleared away from the front of the pool room. We motioned him inside, and all three of us leaned against the bar where we could watch the door.

Fritz said, "The doctor says that he was hit some time last night he thinks. The bullet just nicked a shoulder muscle and all it did was stiffen his left arm."

I said, "What in hell do you expect? I was shooting at a running man and all there was for light was the moon."

Fritz figured it out. "Then Pappas was, the guy that was with the guy that you killed last night?"

"Sure! I figure I winged him because he stumbled. I knew it was either Harold or this Greek. It wasn't Fats Mitchell because the man wasn't that big. So it had to be either Pappas or Harold."

Fritz said, "Why did Pappas take that punk kid with him then? Why didn't Harold go?"

I said, "Don't be silly! Pappas was doing a little double-crossing. I figured that either he or Fats or Harold would get that idea, so I fixed it so the word about the money would go around. Any of those three would have done it; the only thing, Pappas was the one that thought of it. I'll bet that Fats and Harold don't know that he was creased. When his double-cross petered out, he figured he might as well play with Fats and Harold in the original deal."

Kendricks said, "We can find out. Here they are."

The two of them were just pulling into the curb. Kendricks slid over to stand next to the door, where they'd have to pass him, and I said to Fritz:

"Keep out of this, guy! Get down to the back of the place, quick."

The front of the place wasn't going to be too healthy for anyone that didn't know the score and I wanted Fritz away.

He didn't move for a moment and then, by the time he'd gotten in action, he'd only time to get a few feet away when Fats and Harold came in through the door.

They were both empty handed and I remember looking at the clock right above them, right over the door. It read a quarter to six. They saw me standing there but entirely missed Kendricks. All they had eyes for was me. They looked past me and saw Fritz then and I saw Fats wet his lips with the end of his tongue.

Harold started it with: "Well, it's the city slicker, Fats."

I said, "What did you do with Wilson's dough? You got it with you, ain't you? You figured to put it in the big safe here, didn't you? Is it on you or hid in the car?"

Fats said, "The guy is nuts, Harold."

I said, "Will you stand a frisk?"

Fritz came back then and butted in with: "Fats, you and Harold had better come down to the station with me. If you're in the clear it won't hurt you; if you're not, that's where you'll end." And then the damn fool kept on walking. Kept on until he got between those two and myself.

If Fats and Harold had known Kendricks was behind them they might have taken it quietly. But they didn't know that and Fats had a lot of faith in his local pull. He probably thought he could claim self-defense, or that I was trying to hold up his place. And he knew his Mayor brother-in-law angle would keep Fritz's mouth shut, after the thing was over and done. He jerked Fritz ahead and toward him and shouted at Harold at the same time:

"Take him, Harold!"

Harold tried. He deserves credit. He yanked at a gun he carried in his back pocket and I shot him in his right shoulder before he ever got it from under his coat tails. Fritz was acting as a shield for Fats Mitchell. He didn't want to be, but Fats had one big fat arm around him and was hugging him up close. Fats had gotten a gun out from someplace, and he was trying to line this on me. He wasn't doing so well because Fritz was trying to get away from the bear hug and was jerking him around.

Then I saw Kendricks step behind Fats and bring the barrel of his gun along Fats' jaw. Fats went down, taking Fritz with him, and I took Harold's gun out of his back pocket.

That's all there was to that. Harold had the money stuck inside his shirt. Loose. Just a shirt full of big bills. Fritz got up and called the ambulance for Harold, and called the station for the kid cop that followed the Chief around. The kid cop and the ambulance arrived together and Kendricks said to the kid:

"You ride the ambulance up with this bird. And then you live in his hospital room with him until he's able to be moved to the jail. You get it?"

The kid said he got it and rode away. Fritz started out with Fats Mitchell for the station. All he could say was: "Will the Mayor's nose be out of joint!"

We watched them go and Kendricks said, "I guess that clears it up. What you going to do now?"

I said, "Wait for Wilson. Linda was going to leave the lodge and pick him up. At six."

Kendricks looked up at the clock and said, "She'll leave in five minutes then."

It was five to six. The blow-off had come and gone in ten minutes. Kendricks went on with: "That Linda's a swell little girl. I've noticed you thought so too. I don't wish anybody hard luck, but I wouldn't feel too bad if Fats and Harold had worked Wilson over a bit when they took his dough. I've been off that bird ever since he ran over the Wop kid. For that matter, I used to go hunting with that guide he killed."

I said, "Why, mister! That guide was shot accidentally. He was fooling with Wilson's gun and it went off."

Kendricks said, "I bet Wilson was holding it when it did, too."

I said, "Well, his luck won't hold always. Sometime he'll have one of these accidents where there's witnesses around."

LINDA GOT IN town a few minutes after six. I saw their big sedan make the turn from the lodge road and down in front of the police station, and saw Wilson get out. Kendricks and I were on the sidewalk, in front of Fats Mitchell's pool room. I shouted at Wilson and waved my hat. He started walking up the street toward me, and Kendricks and I started toward him. Linda stayed in the car.

Wilson was probably a hundred feet from us when the Italian, Pacelli, stepped from some store about half-way between us. He turned and faced Wilson and started down the sidewalk toward him. His hands were in plain sight and empty.

Wilson stopped stock still. I said to Kendrick, "Say! That's the father of the girl he ran over, ain't it?"

Kendrick said it was and we kept on walking. We didn't hurry; had no reason to hurry as far as we knew. But when Pacelli got within about ten feet of Wilson, Wilson cried out: "Stay back, you!"

Wilson had a permit to carry a gun and he'd been carrying one since he'd been threatened. I'd known this, but didn't think anything about it at that moment. Pacelli said something, what it was I couldn't hear, and Wilson whipped out this damn gun and leveled it.

Kendricks and I were about twenty feet behind Pacelli, who was standing on the inside of the sidewalk. Wilson was on the outside, where I could see him. Pacelli had his legs spread wide apart; I don't suppose he had any idea of what was going to happen, and his hands were hanging by his side. I braked to a stop just as Pacelli put his hand out toward Wilson, and I heard Pacelli say:

"Now wait, Mister Wilson! I—"

Wilson's face showed he meant to shoot. He looked like a crazy man. I didn't know it but I'd hauled my gun out and was ready. Wilson set himself for his gun's recoil and squinted a bit, and I brought my gun up and lined it on his shoulder. I could see from Wilson's face that he was taking up the slack in his trigger and then, right at the side of his shoulder I saw the big sedan with Linda in the front seat.

She was right in line. I was coming back on the trigger when I saw this and I twitched the muzzle just as the gun rocked back in my hand. The slug caught Wilson just by his nose. I could see the hole it made. He dropped the arm that held his gun, straight down, as though he had no elbow joint and the arm was in one piece. Then he folded down on the sidewalk.

Kendricks got to Wilson first. I stopped by Pacelli and said. "You got a gun on you?"

He still didn't realize what had happened. All he knew was that he'd been looking at a man holding and pointing a gun at him and that the man had fallen on the sidewalk.

He said, "No. I no got gun. I not own gun."

I said, "Fine. Stand here. Don't move. I'm going to need an out."

Kendricks turned his head and said, "Need an out, hell! The town will chip in and buy you a medal. This guy would have shot that poor Wop in his tracks if you hadn't stepped in."

By that time Linda was there. I was afraid to look at her. She stopped by her stepfather and Kendricks said, "Don't look, Miss Wilson. I'm afraid your father's dead."

She came to me then. She said, "Shean! Did you have to kill him?"

I said, "If I'd shot him through the shoulder, the slug would probably have gone through him and hit you, in the car. I couldn't take the chance. If I hadn't shot he'd have murdered Pacelli."

She started to cry and sobbed out that Wilson had been

crazy; that somebody along the road had called out to him to drop the money and that he'd done this. And that he'd told her he was certain it was Pacelli who'd called. She argued that he'd been insane from fear since he'd started getting the threatening letters and that he'd lived in terror of Pacelli since the time he'd run over Pacelli's little girl.

I said, "It was three of the local talent sending the letters. If your dad hadn't gone hillbilly on us it would have been all over. The locals are in the hospital and the jail."

Kendricks said, "He must have been crazy. What do you mean he went hillbilly?"

I said, "He was feuding. With Pacelli. Only Pacelli didn't know it."

THE CORONER'S INQUEST was a joke. They found that Wilson came to his death while of unsound mind and at the hands of Shean Connell. Shean Connell was absolved of any blame in the affair. Three of the six men on the coroner's jury came over to me and muttered something about: "Pacelli is a credit to the town," and the other three mentioned that Wilson was no good and that the world was better off without him. Even Dan, the bartender that had run me out of his place, shook hands with me.

Fritz, the policeman, was wrong about the entire town turning out for Wilson's funeral. The town wasn't represented by anybody but the Mayor. After it was all over and Linda and I were back on the lodge porch she said:

"I'm glad it's over. I suppose I should feel bad but I don't. All he did was throw Mother's money away and chase after cheap women." Then she stopped and looked me over and added: "I know where you were those evenings you said you had business in town. You were playing the piano in one of those *places.*"

"What was I going to do? I had to find out things and that's the only night life a small town has. That was about the only place I could dig up information. You want to remember that my friend, Beck, was killed right outside the place where I worked. That was the logical place to look for his killer."

"But you were working for Dad."

"Murder's murder, honey! The poor guy was from my agency and I wanted to clear the slate for him."

"Well, you did."

"I did. Kendricks tells me the slugs they took out of Beck came from Harold's gun, so that cinches the murder on Harold. I figured it was one of those three but didn't know which one. He shot at you and me, too.... Are you sore about my piano playing in that place?"

"I don't like it very much."

Mrs. Wilson came to the door and smiled at us and went back inside. She looked a lot brighter and happier since they'd taken her husband away in the hearse; Linda told me that Wilson had always given her mother hell.

Then Linda said, "We're going to the city. We live at 21 West Pacific."

"I'll remember that."

"You're going to call, then?"

"The only way anybody could keep me away from 21 West Pacific would be to lock me in my room."

She grinned and said there was always fire-escapes in case anything like that happened. Then we kept right on talking... but not about fire-escapes.

Just a Nice Girl

Hired guns blast an alibi

HE CAME OVER to me before I'd been in the Sunshine Club an hour. The place has a long horseshoe bar, very gaudy, and I was right at the bend. He was carrying a highball glass as though he was afraid he might lose his balance and spill a drop. He sat next to me and said:

"You're Shean Connell, aren't you?"

I said I was, and suggested he put his glass on the bar before both he and his glass fell off his stool. He minded me and kept on with:

"The Connell that's a cop, I mean?"

There was no reason for it being a secret and I told him I had a private license. He grunted, tilted part of his drink down without spilling much and then said:

"That's fine. I got something for you and I've been looking for you. I called your agency and they said I might find you here. So I asked the barman and he pointed you out."

He stopped then, fumbled in his pocket for a big brown manilia envelope, handed this to me.

"It's for you to keep," he said. "It's my insurance policies. There's an order, notarized, giving you the authority to investigate my death. There's a thousand-dollar check for a retainer, and the executors of my estate have instructions to pay you the balance of your fee when you earn it"

Then he took the rest of his drink and stood. I got him by the arm and said, "Sit down!" and because I'm some bigger, he did. I said, "What is this?"

"It's just that I want you to investigate my death, Mr. Connell."

"But you aren't dead."

He looked at me hazily, but still in the eye, and said, "No, but I will be."

The talk about the thousand-dollar check had me interested. The Sunshine Club bar has booths, nice deep ones, and I got away from my stool, taking him with me, and headed toward one of these. I sat him down, he was rubber-legged, and got across from him, and said:

"Now you better begin at the beginning. What's this about insurance and thousand-dollar checks? Start from the first."

"It's the finish for me, not the starting. It's like this, Connell. I've got a business. Wholesale groceries. I inherited it. I've got a

partner. I've got a half-brother. I've been married and divorced and have an ex-wife. I married again and am separated from my second wife. Now do you see?"

I didn't see and said so. I'd been sizing him up while he talked. He was about thirty, the long, tall, thin type, and he was drunker than a skunk. But a serious drunk, not the drinking-for-a-good-time kind of drunk. He had blond hair, already getting thin on top and away from his forehead, and he had a sort of droopy discouraged look around the mouth. He wore good clothes, but he looked as though he'd slept in them for a couple of days. Altogether, a decent looking sort of man.

I said again that I didn't understand and then: "What d'ya mean it's the finish for you?"

He beckoned the waiter and ordered drinks, waited until they came, then said:

"It's just this. Late last night somebody tried to kill me. Shot at me three times and missed. The only reason for anybody to kill me is the insurance I carry. Forty thousand to my partner and the same to my half-brother. Fifty thousand to each of my wives. Now do you see?"

I said I began to get the idea.

"It's just that I don't want anybody that kills me to profit by it. That's all. I don't mind being killed so much, but I don't want whoever does it to collect on my insurance."

It began to look as though the man was a bit off. I said, "Now look! I don't even know your name."

"Terwilliger. Andrew S. Terwilliger."

"I don't understand this at all. Why don't you hire me to find out who tried to kill you? When I do it, you can cancel out that particular insurance policy. That's reasonable, and this idea of waiting until you're dead to start to work isn't. When you sober up, suppose you come around to the office and we'll talk this over."

He put his drink down and leaned across the table, and he talked as though he'd never had a drink in his life. "It's like this, Mr. Connell. I don't really mind if somebody gets me out of the way. I don't really care about it. The doctor tells me I'll be dead inside of six months, if I keep drinking, so it really doesn't matter."

"And you were really shot at?"

"I really was, Mr. Connell. Three times in front of my apartment house. From a closed car, parked across the street. The bullet marks are plainly in evidence, on the front of the building, and the police made an immediate investigation. You may check this if you're in doubt, Mr. Connell."

"What about me taking you home? Right now."

He straightened and looked dignified and said he wouldn't dream of allowing me to do this. That he had his usual night-clubbing yet to do and that he expected to be carried home at his usual time, which was when the bars closed. And I watched him go out and I put the envelope in my pocket and thought: "Just another young fool with too much money in his pocket and too much liquor in his belly."

I thought he'd be around to the office in the morning to explain what screwy thing was in his mind. That is, until a few minutes later, when I got ready to leave. Frank, the barman, was in front of me, and he leaned over the plank and said:

"Nice young fella, that Andy Terwilliger."

"I thought he was nuts, myself."

Frank shook his head as though at something very sad. "He will be nuts, Mr. Connell, he will be. He's in love with his first wife yet. She quit him and he married another girl to forget her. This second one quits him, too. Now he can't make up his mind whether he loves the first one or the second one the most, and he's trying to drink the bars dry to forget both of them. He's doing first class on this drying up the bars, too. That is, for a green hand. And I was talking to Halper, that's a cop that comes in now and then, and Hal tells me somebody tried to bump the kid last night. Hal didn't know why, but he said somebody tried to kill him, all right."

I said, " 'Night, Frank!" and left. I caught a cab and started to make the rounds of the night spots looking for my new client. Frank had said enough to make me a believer.

THE METER WAS up to nine dollars and eighty cents by three o'clock and I was tired out, but I was still a believer. But I believed that Andrew S. Terwilliger was a smarter man than I was; he knew places to go that I didn't. I'd been to every place in town that I knew; had run into them a few minutes or a few hours after he had, but I was still behind. I'd found his house phone number in the book and had called in there every few minutes, but he hadn't gone home. At three I came out of the last place way over at the edge of town and said to the cabby:

"Take me to the Central Police Station."

The hacker looked back at the meter and knocked the flag up and said, "Now listen, chief. That clock ain't wrong. But you been a good customer and I'll go even with you. Let the station go, what d'ya say? It just makes trouble for you and me both."

I said: "You dope! Take me to the station. I got more on my mind than you and your damned meter."

He hunched his head down and drove, and when we got there I climbed out and said, "Wait for me!"

"Geeze, chief, I'll get it checked in the morning. So help me, I will."

I said, "You wait for me," and went inside.

Charley Evans was on the desk, and he grinned at me and said, "Hi, Shean! What's the matter, can't you sleep?"

"There's a guy named Terwilliger running around loose," I said. "I hear he got shot at last night and I'm worried about him. Will you check up on it?"

He leaned back and tried to look as though he was a police judge instead of a police sergeant. "What's it all about, Shean?"

I said I wished that I knew. He gave me more of his magistrate act and said, "Now look, Shean! What's behind it, that's what we want to know? Three bullets chipped pieces of wall right above this guy last night, and when we brought him down here he said he didn't have any idea what the shooting was for. You can't call that cooperation, Shean, you know you can't. Who's after the guy and why?"

I said, "As near as I can figure out, all his relatives. Those by marriage and the other. And his partner. Though, seeing I just met him tonight for the first time, and seeing that I didn't talk to him for more than five minutes, and seeing that he was stiffer than a plank at the time, I'm not sure of anything. I don't even know the names of these relatives and partners and all."

He said he could tell me that and I asked him how he knew. He said a cop, Lou Halper, had checked the shooting and got curious about it and checked the relative and partner angle just for fun. He got on the telephone and finally managed to get a sleepy clerk to dig up a report that told me Terwilliger's partner was named John Hempstead and lived at 3314 Jerboe Road, and that his half-brother was named Laurence Terwilliger and lived well down on Eleventh Avenue.

I said, "Hempstead lives out where the swells do, and the half-brother lives among the bums."

Charley Evans said, "That's right. And this half-brother has a record. Armed assault once and once for selling fake oil stock. He's even been vagged a couple of times."

I kept on looking and saw that Terwilliger's first wife was

named Martha and lived on Celeste Boulevard and that the second was named Janet and lived on East 54th. Both good addresses.

"Is that all Lou Halper could dig up? Lou's a pretty good man; if he was really curious he ought to have been able to find out more than that."

Charley looked at the ceiling and said, "That's about all. Though some pigeon told him Fat Dillon was around the neighborhood where the shooting took place. Though I'll always say, if Fat Dillon did the shooting, Terwilliger would be dead as a smelt, right now."

"Damn you, Charley," I said. "Why didn't you tell me that? You know damn well Dillon will hire out to anybody with dough."

I started out the door and he called after me: "You going to talk to Dillon?"

"That's right."

"You know where he lives?"

I stopped and said: "The Martinez Hotel. He owns it."

Charley said, "You do know at that."

"I should, Charley. I played piano for him in that basement show he had during prohibition. Before I got honest and turned copper, that was."

He grinned and said, "That kills me; a private cop being honest. Oh, well, if you know Dillon, he'll talk to you."

I said, "He maybe will. I had to beat his fat face in when I quit. To get the money I had coming. He'll talk or else."

I started out again and just as I was closing the door he called: "I'll send flowers if it's 'or else.' "

FAT DILLON WAS an old-time Barbary Coaster who hadn't let new times and old age creep up on him. He was a big paunchy fat man, maybe sixty, and it was reported that in the old days he'd kill a man for a ten-dollar bill. He'd changed; I didn't think he'd do the job now for less than a hundred. He owned a fourth-class hotel in the tough district, and I'd played piano for what he'd called a 'floor show' in the honky-tonk he'd run in the basement. I'd called it other names and so had the police, the dozen or more times they'd closed it.

Dillon was money hungry; the tightest man I'd ever met. If anybody waved money at him he couldn't say no, and I guess it was a paying policy. He'd bought the hotel that way, at least. He wouldn't hesitate to use crooked dice in a two-bit crap game, not even if he had a million dollars in his pockets. He hated me and I thought as much of him. I got out to the curb and the hacker gave me a scared look and said:

"See, chief! I waited, didn't I?"

I said, "Sure. You still got that nine eighty on the clock. You had to wait."

"Geeze, chief! I thought you was going in to make a squawk about that nine eighty. Honest, I did."

"Get going. The Martinez Hotel."

He got going. When we got within about four blocks of the hotel, he twisted around in his seat and said in a worried voice:

"Say, chief, you know what kind of a joint this Martinez is?"

"I do."

"I hate to see you go in there, chief. You know what I mean; it's a joint. You'll come out of there clipped to the skin."

"You mean you want your nine eighty before I go in, because you think I might not have it coming out. Isn't that it?"

He said that wasn't the idea at all; that he made a practice of looking out for his customers. Right then we pulled into the place and I paid him off, tipped him two bucks, and said:

"O.K., run along."

I heard the music as soon as I stepped on the sidewalk, and the basement entrance to the so-called café was still lit by the Neon sign that read: *Dillon's*. I went down the stairs and in, and saw Fat Dillon behind the bar and peering into the cash register. I stopped right inside the door and watched him. He'd count money for a moment, then look over at his bartender and scowl. Then the same thing again, only he'd look toward the two waiters. There were three couples on the floor, two of them far too drunk even to try to dance. There were possibly half a dozen more in the booths around the place. They had a piano, banjo, and drums, for music, and the piano player knew me and called over:

"Hi, Shean!"

I called back: "Hi, Mitch!" and went over to the bar.

Dillon got away from the register and leaned his fat arms on the bar. I said I'd take a rye, straight, and he looked at the clock and said, "Too late, Connell," in a sour voice.

I said, "O.K., Fat! I'd rather have it with you, up in your room, anyway. Suppose you ask me up."

He had tiny, hard little eyes, and the fat on his face was so heavy you could hardly see them. He blinked them, once, almost whispered: "What is it, Connell? What is it?"

"Terwilliger," I said, and I made it just as low.

He didn't move a muscle, just stared back at me. Mitchell, the piano player, called over: "Want to sit in for a number, Shean?"

I called back: "Maybe later," and kept watching Dillon.

Then Dillon said, in this same whisper: "Go sit in for a couple of tunes. Then come up to my room—402. Third floor, right in front. I'll be waiting for you."

He turned back to the register and I went over to the piano and ribbed Mitchell for a few minutes. Mitchell claimed business was lousy and that he was just making his four-dollar-a-night guarantee, and I told him that was three more than he was entitled to get for working in a lousy joint like that. He said he'd seen the day and many of them when I'd have been glad to work for room and fodder in worse places and I said there were no worse places.

All in fun. I sat in then and played three old-timers and got stuck on a request number that had come out since I'd quit the business, so I gave the piano back to Mitchell, and eased through the door that led upstairs into the hotel proper. The clerk looked asleep, the one bellboy just about. He started toward the elevator, but I pointed at the stairs and said:

"I know the way."

"Yes, Mr. Connell," he said. "Mr. Dillon said you'd be up."

Then I started up.

I wasn't quite sure what I was going against. If Dillon was mixed with the attempt to kill Terwilliger, he might be dangerous. If he knew anything about it, he'd talk. For money. That is, if his own skirts were in the clear. I was in his own place, with his own hired help around, and if there was trouble and anything happened to me, they could swear him out of it. Particularly as we'd had trouble before. It was about an even bet there'd be trouble, I thought, so I went up the stairs very slowly and quietly, and with my gun out and ready.

He could have figured me as riding the elevator and be waiting for me by that door. And he could be thinking I'd play safe and walk the stairs, and be waiting for me around the next turn.

There was a third angle, too. Outside of Fat Dillon being seen around where the Terwilliger shooting attempt had taken place, there was nothing to connect him with Terwilliger at all. But I knew Dillon would never leave his bar cash register alone, unless he had a chance to make more outside than the register would take in. So the third angle didn't worry me much; nothing but money would ever get Dillon away from the Martinez and I knew it, and there was money behind the Terwilliger business.

I was on the second floor landing and peeking up the stairs toward the third when the shooting started. A big gun, and somebody was spacing the shots out: *One... two... three.* Three shots. They were muffled, but there was no mistaking what they were; no mistaking the heavy slamming boom a .44 or .45 caliber gun makes in a room with the door closed.

Then a door slammed and feet pounded in the corridor above me. I went up the stairs, three at a time, and I got the third floor door open just in time to see somebody running down the hall, almost at the back of the house.

I shouted, "Stop! Stop, you!"

Whoever it was didn't stop but put on more speed. I chased after him, not wanting to shoot. I didn't know who it was or what the shooting had been about or who'd done the shooting. He reached the end of the hall before I'd got well started, and when I got to the backstairs door he'd gone through, it was locked. It looked flimsy and wasn't. I tried to break it with my shoulder, once, before I remembered Dillon always reinforced his doors with iron, because of the added time it would give him to clean house in case of a police raid. So I turned and went back down the hall.

Dillon's door was closed, and I knocked, standing well to the side. Nobody answered. I reached over and tried the door and the knob turned easily, letting the door swing in a couple of inches.

And then I braced myself and went in, fast, not knowing whether I was going into the finish of the shooting match I'd heard or just what.

LIGHTS WERE ON and the first thing I saw in that room were feet. Big feet. They were sticking out from behind an old-fashioned Morris chair, one of the wooden-framed, leather-backed things that are adjustable. I peeked around the chair and saw they belonged to Fat Dillon, who was very dead. He was lying on his side, and a slug had caught him in the face, just at the side of his nose. Another had caught him under the chin. There was a bloody spot high on the left side of his white shirt, which made three times and out. In spite of the blood on his face he looked surprised, startled. Then someone said, from behind me:

"H-h-h-hands up, M-m-mister!"

I turned around and saw the clerk, who'd been asleep when I started up. He was holding a little cheap, nickel-plated pistol in his hand and the pistol was pointing all around the room. He was shaking that much. His face was greenish-white, and he took the hand that wasn't shimmying with the pistol and pointed at Fat Dillon's feet and said:

"You killed him. You killed Mr. Dillon."

He talked a lot better this time. His stutter was gone and he started to hold the pistol so it lined on me instead of the four corners of the room. I reached out and took the pistol away from him and said:

"Give me that! What in hell d'ya mean, I killed Mr. Dillon?"

From where he was, all he could see were feet. I wanted to find out how he knew they belonged to Dillon. He gulped a couple of times, then said, "Those feet are Mr. Dillon's. I know it."

"How?"

"I—I recognize his shoes."

The bellboy padded up behind him then and he turned and screeched, "Get the police, Sam. This man has killed Mr. Dillon."

I said, "Sam! Get in here. You know me."

Sam knew me and minded. He came in. I made them both stand in one corner of the room, looked around, and sized things up, and Sam said, "You better get the hell outta here, Mr. Connell! The cops'll be here any time."

"Shut up," I said. "There isn't anybody registered in this scatter of Dillon's that wants to see the cops bad enough to call them. Don't be a dope."

"They'll hear the shots from the streets."

"Did you hear 'em downstairs?"

"Sure. Three of 'em. Boom, boom, boom!"

"Did you know they came from here?"

"Well, Mr. Smith said, 'Connell's killed Mr. Dillon,' and grabbed the gun that's behind the desk and started running up the stairs. I just followed him. I didn't know the shooting was here; I just knew it was upstairs is all. But Mr. Smith knew."

I'd been looking around the room. There wasn't a thing in it except a few gun-slinging Western magazines, a half-empty bottle of dollar whiskey, and some dirty shirts in a dresser drawer. And, of course, Fat Dillon. And then I saw the gun, lying under the Morris chair and by Dillon's hand. Just where it would have gone if he'd dropped it when he fell. I didn't move it. I turned to this clerk, who was shaking all over, and said:

"Your name's Smith, is that it?"

"Yes, sir. Smith. Wilbur Smith."

"How long you worked here, Wilbur?"

"About three months. Between three and four months."

"How'd you know my name?"

"Why, Sam told me, I guess."

Sam said indignantly, "Why I did no such thing. I knew Mr. Connell when he played downstairs, but I never told you about him."

Smith said to me, "I—I guess it was Mr. Dillon that told me."

I said, "I guess it was," and opened the closet door, and a body almost fell on me before I could jump back out of the way.

It was quite stiff. It fell forward on its face, but because it had been doubled up a bit in the closet, it looked as though it was trying to stand on its head for a second. Then it teetered over and fell on its side, and I saw the face and said:

"The copper! Lou Halper!"

Then I heard the snarling sound a police siren makes and it didn't sound as though it was more than two blocks away. I said to Sam:

"Be seeing you," and to Smith: "You too, Wilbur," and took the key from the inside of the door. I locked it from the outside and, knowing either Sam or Wilbur would surely have a pass-key in their pockets, I left the key half turned in the lock.

Then I took out for the fire-escape in the back. It looked as though I wouldn't be able to shake the cops for a minute, and I couldn't waste time blabbing to them. I was level with the first floor when the police car pulled up in front and the siren died away with a little moaning noise. I was at the landing that swings down when I heard one of the cops open the side gate that led into the walk around the hotel, and I got to the back door of the next building just as he rounded the corner, with his flashlight showing him the way.

The cops were working the way they should; going in front and back. He tried the back door of the hotel, jumped inside, and I tried the back door of my building and didn't do as good. It was locked but the shadow of it had covered me from the flashlight.

I got away and into the alley, and heard another siren come howling up as I did. I went down the alley as fast as I could, got half-way the length of it, and tied up with a barking, growling alley cur that I'd have cheerfully throttled if I could have got my hands on it.

This kept with me until I got to the end of the alley. The police car passed the end of the alley just before I got to it, but they were going too fast to hear the noise the pup made, so I peeked out on the street and looked around.

There was a car parked just down the street, and I could see a man and girl in it. I got to them, opened the door of the car and jammed my gun into their faces. They quit kissing each other and the girl screamed and said:

"Ooh, hon! A hold-up!"

I said to her, "Move over!" and to the man: "Get this crate going and get out of here. Drive slow. I'll tell you when to stop."

He looked undecided, then at the gun, then put his foot on the starter.

And that was that. Another police car passed us before we were four blocks away, but they didn't even look our way. And I got out of the car where an arcade cut through a building. I didn't head for my hotel. I knew Wilbur Smith, the night clerk, had already started talking, and there'd be cops waiting to welcome me home.

LINDA WILSON LIVED in Brentwood Heights and I made the trip in three cabs. I thought I could hole up at her house. I'd dated her enough in the past month to merit a hide-out there. I got to her place about eight-thirty in the morning, and if I looked the way I felt, she shouldn't have let me in the house. I'd known her since I'd broken a case for her stepfather and she liked me, even though this stepfather had accidentally got himself killed during the case. I stood inside the door and she looked me over and said:

"My word, Shean! What is it? What's the matter? What's happened, honey?"

I said, "Unless I'm wrong, the police are looking for me with their thousand eyes. Or is it the night that's supposed to have a thousand eyes? I think I'm supposed to have killed a hoodlum named Fat Dillon. And a dead policeman named Lou Halper was in the same room with Dillon and I'll maybe be blamed for that, too."

"But Shean, that's terrible!"

" 'That's terrible' is a miracle of understatement. If the cops think I killed Officer Halper, they'll really go to town on me. A cop killer don't get a break, not in this or any man's town."

"But honey, what's it all about?"

I said I didn't know; that the thing started over a drunk named Terwilliger. That Terwilliger had been shot at and that I had the notion Fat Dillon might know something about it. And that Lou Halper probably had the same hunch, or maybe even something to go on. And then I remembered I still had the envelope Terwilliger had given me and that I hadn't opened it.

I said, "Look, Linda! I'm hungry. I'm tired. Could you get me something to eat and keep me out of sight until I can get a little rest and think of some way out of this mess."

She said, "I'll tell cook to get something under way right this minute."

"Don't tell cook anything. She may know other cooks and talk to them about me. You'll have to do it some other way. You realize it's going to make trouble for you if I'm found here, don't you? The police don't like people that hide criminals."

She put her nose in the air and said I was no criminal and that she'd love to hide me. And then: "Breakfast won't be until nine. I'll have cook make me a tray and bring it upstairs. The spare room is right next to my bedroom, and you could stay in there a week and no one would know it. Not even Mother would know it."

"She wouldn't like this, hon."

"She wouldn't care, Shean. Mother likes you, too. Lots."

I said, "Is it just 'like' now, hon?" and she got red in the face and took my hand and led me upstairs. She put me in the spare room, with a key to the door, and I said, "I'd sure like to see the morning paper, too."

"O.K.," she said. "I've got the order."

The paper came up with the breakfast and the coffee got cold while Linda and I read how I was wanted for the murder of Horace Dillon, a known underworld figure, and Louis Halper, a city detective. This was the first I'd known Fat's first name had been Horace; if I'd known it while I worked for him I'd have ribbed the pants off his fat behind. The police promised an early arrest, as usual, and Chief of Detectives Vorley even intimated the police had me bottled up in some mysterious place. There was nothing said about Terwilliger, or the case having anything to do with him, but there were pictures of Wilbur Smith, a clerk in Dillon's hotel who'd "been threatened by the killer" and of Sam, the bellboy, who'd been treated the same way. There were statements by them. Also from the couple I'd kidnaped. The girl said, "I can hardly believe it possible. The man acted very gentlemanly and treated me with great respect." The guy said, "I knew he was a killer the moment I saw his glaring eyes." Linda thought this last one very funny and said, "Glare at me, Shean."

I was reading where the entire force had been thrown into the search for me and didn't feel so good. And the Terwilliger business didn't make any more sense than it had before when I opened the letter he'd given me. There were the four policies he'd told me about. There was a letter authorizing me to act as his agent, or rather his estate's agent in the event of his death. Just as he'd said. And the thousand-dollar check, which I had a fat chance of cashing the way things were. Linda looked these over with me and said:

"Why, I know Janet Terwilliger. I knew her before she was married. Somehow, I never connected her with the Terwilliger you were working for."

It seemed that Janet, Terwilliger's second wife, was a lively girl and that Linda was crazy about her. But that they'd just lost track of each other, the way people do. That Janet was certainly not the type to have her husband killed in order to collect on his insurance policy. Quite a lot more of this.

I didn't bother to tell her that very often nice people were mixed up in murder cases and other major crimes. After all, she still had illusions. And I was too tired to want to talk, even to her.

I must have gone to sleep within five minutes from the time she left me.

Linda woke me up about four o'clock that afternoon. She knocked on the door with a little double-knock, and I let her in and she held out a newspaper to me and said:

"Look, Shean!"

This time I read where I'd been seen in six different places, hundreds of miles apart. But that wasn't what she meant. Andrew S. Terwilliger, the man I was supposed to be working for, had been picked up a few blocks from the Martinez Hotel, by one of the police cars first on the scene. The police had kept him out of sight while they worked on him, but he'd finally got word out to his lawyer who'd got him out on a writ. I said to Linda:

"That'll be Charley Evans, the night desk man. Charley must have remembered what Halper was working on when he got killed and passed the word along. If not, they'd have turned Terwilliger loose when he proved his identity."

"What do you think he was doing down there?"

I said I didn't know.

"Maybe he was the man who shot this Dillon?"

I said maybe he was.

"Maybe he was down there trying to make Dillon confess to who hired him. Terwilliger might know that Dillon had shot at him, and wanted to make Dillon tell."

I thought of Fat Dillon and just what a tough egg he'd been, then thought of Terwilliger and what a drunk he'd been the only time I saw him. This didn't fit and I said so. I said, "He might have gone off the deep end, in a drunken moment, and tried to kill Dillon. That's possible. Anything's possible to a drunk sometimes. But I don't think a man could get drunk enough to think he could make Dillon talk. Dillon was a cold-blooded professional killer, hon, and that kind don't talk."

"You were going to make him talk."

"I was going to try and show him it would pay him to talk. That's different."

A maid came up calling: "Miss Linda! Miss Linda!"

Linda sighed and said, "I guess it's somebody calling. Try and sleep again, Shean. I thought you'd want to know about Terwilliger."

I said, "I want to know a lot about Terwilliger. That's my one aim in life now."

She left and I locked the door after her.

She was back inside of five minutes with her double-knock. She slipped inside, her eyes looking wide and startled, and said:

"Shean! It's a policeman. What will you do?"

I asked who the policeman was.

"It's a man named Lieutenant Arnold. A big, slow-talking blond man."

"I know him. Homicide Detail."

"He said he knew you were here and for me to tell you he'd wait for you. I said you weren't here and that I hadn't seen you, and he just smiled at me and said that he'd wait. That's what he's doing; waiting."

I said, "O.K., hon! I might as well get it over with. I might have known the cops would know we were running around together. That's the first thing they'd check."

Arnold was parked in a big chair and looked happy and comfortable. The maid had brought him a drink in a long tall glass and he was sipping this and smoking a cigar as big as the drink. He grinned at me and said:

"Hello, Shean! I thought the little lady was holding you out of circulation. What's the idea?"

"I wanted time to do a little checking, Arnie."

"Well, go ahead and take it. That's what I want to see you about."

"A lot of checking I'll be able to do in a cell."

He waved both the glass and the cigar at me and said, "Don't be silly. Did you kill Halper?"

"No."

"Well, we know that. Halper had been dead for about ten hours when he was found. You had an alibi for that time. I know; I checked it."

"I was in no shape to check alibis, Arnie. I figured you guys wouldn't be in any shape to listen to reason."

He lost his grin and admitted they hadn't been, not at the time they'd found Halper's body. And then:

"What about Dillon?"

I told him what had happened and he listened, cocking his head to one side when I came to the part about the hotel clerk. He said, "For that matter, whoever killed Dillon did the world a favor. But you can see how it would look to a jury, Shean."

I said, "Oh, nuts. Take me down and get it over with. Why rub it in?"

"I'm not going to take you down. That's why I was looking for you."

"What's this stuff in the paper about a general alarm being out for me."

He grinned. "That was my idea. Whoever did the killing will be resting easy, thinking we're only after you. I think that was a smart move."

Linda started to cry then and I had five minutes out to soothe her down. Then, when she was better, and had gone upstairs to put back the make-up she'd cried away, Arnold said:

"Now what about Terwilliger?"

"I'd like to know. I'm just where I started. Don't know a thing more."

Arnold said, very softly, "Terwilliger lives about two blocks from here. Does that give you any ideas, Mister Shean?"

I said: "We'll have to wait until dark."

ARNOLD WOULD HAVE made a good burglar, if he hadn't been a better policeman. Linda had gone shopping for me, and I took the glass cutter she'd acquired and got through a cellar window that night while Arnold did sentry duty for me at the corner of Terwilliger's house. I went in first and Arnold followed me, having a hard time getting his heavy shoulders through the window. He whispered, "Terwilliger is mixed up in this someway. Somebody is working for or against him, and that's why Lou Halper was killed. Now if it's him that's responsible, I'm going to work him over whether he's a client of yours or not."

I said, "Shut up, Arnie. We've been through all that. Come on."

We started toward the cellar steps, picking the way with a flashlight Linda had got for me. No trouble at all. The door at the head of the stairs was unlocked and we stepped into a kitchen.

Then the kitchen light snapped on and somebody said from right behind us:

"Stand still, you two."

We didn't; we both turned. And both saw a man and a gun.

The gun was impressive; the man wasn't. The gun was a .45 Colt automatic and it looked as big as a house. The hammer was back and the safety latch was off. The hole in the muzzle looked so big to me that I couldn't tell whether the gun was pointing at me or at Arnold.

The man didn't look so fancy. A little wizened fellow, maybe fifty years old. Not well dressed, but still not exactly shabby. The kind of man you'd meet one minute and forget the next. Arnold's hand went toward his belt, he carried a gun on a belt holster under his coat, and the man with the gun jerked it a little and said:

"Don't do it."

Arnold took his hand away and put both of them up level with his shoulders and the man said that was right and for me to do the same.

I did. Then he said, "And what are you two bozos looking for, may I ask?"

Arnold's face was red and his voice sounded as though he was choking, when he snapped back: "Yes, you can ask. And point that cannon some other way. I'm a police officer, mister.

Put that gun down."

The man laughed. "Police officer, hell. Coming in a cellar window. Police officer! You're a damned burglar and not even a good one. I could hear the whole thing, clear up here."

Arnold gave me a dirty look and I said, "Hell, Arnie, I never claimed to be good on this breaking and entering."

The man said to me, "You didn't claim it and you aren't good. Now what are you guys after?"

I said, "To see Mr. Terwilliger, dope. Why would we be here?"

"I'm asking the questions," he said, in a smug way. And to Arnold: "If you're a cop, you got bracelets on you. Ain't that right?"

Arnold said he was a cop and that naturally he carried handcuffs. He was so mad by then it was all I could do to understand him. The little man smiled at this and said:

"O.K.! Get over and face the wall. Put your hands up on it, just as high as you can reach. Jump, now."

He tightened his finger on the trigger of his gun when we didn't move… so we moved. Not fast, but still a move. Out of the corner of my eye I could see him slip Arnold's cuffs out and snap one side on Arnold's right wrist. And then he jammed the gun into my back and said:

"All right, stupid! Get that arm of yours down here."

I got the other cuff on my left wrist, then he said, "Now we all go in the front room, just like pals. I'm waiting to see Mr. Terwilliger myself."

I got the look Arnold gave me, and said, "Oh, you're taking over Dillon's unfinished business, eh?"

Arnold asked, "What did you do with the help?"

He didn't get an answer. We went in the front of the house

and the little man sat down where he could watch the front door and also us, where he'd parked us on a lounge.

He hadn't taken either my gun or Arnold's, and my right hand was free, where I could reach it under my arm. It would have been a little more awkward for Arnold, because he'd have to twist his left hand out of shape to get at that belt holster of his. So Arnold kept watching me out of the corner of his eye and the little fellow kept watching us both.

I didn't make a move; it didn't look right. And I was right. We got in the house about nine-thirty, and at ten-thirty the little devil said in a disappointed voice:

"So you guys ain't going to make a try for it, huh?"

I said, "A try for what, friend?"

He laughed and came over and started reaching for my gun, holding his own well back and against his hip, where I couldn't possibly reach it.

Arnold reached for it; moving faster than I thought a big man could.

He got it by the muzzle and I got the little man by the other wrist at the same time. The gun banged, but I knew I didn't get hit, though I couldn't tell about Arnold. I jerked the wrist I had my hand on over to where I could put my handcuffed hand on it as well, and then saw Arnold had the gun tipped up. Then it banged again, just as the little man jerked the upper part of his body, and I saw the flame lance up and catch the man in the face.

I let go of the wrist I held. Arnold let go the gun. And the little man let go of everything and just wilted to the floor.

Arnold and I were still sitting on the couch, with the little man on the floor in front of us. Arnold turned his head toward me and said:

"My Gawd, Connell! I was never so scared in my life. The little —— just sat there, waiting for one of us to try and make a play for a gun. He just sat there and waited for us. What a guy. Just cat and mouse stuff."

"He was waiting for Terwilliger to come home, to kill him. Maybe he thought he needed practice."

Arnold fished his handcuff key out and tried to smile. "One thing, Connell. The town is gradually cleaning up over this mess. First Dillon, then this bird."

He searched the little man then, finding one thousand and twenty-eight dollars in currency and a little silver. And a spare clip for the .45 automatic. And a slip of paper with Terwilliger's name and address on it. Arnold showed this to me, and I saw it was on the back of an envelope addressed to Mr. J. Swope, with an address on Tenth Avenue. Then Arnold handed me a key that was lettered: Martinez Hotel.

"It's got no room number on it," Arnold said.

I said, "Lot's of times pass-keys haven't. What did you do with Smith?"

"Turned him loose."

"Does he live at the hotel or just work there?"

"He lives on Tenth Avenue." Arnold looked at the envelope again, added slowly: "That's what's familiar with this enve-lope. The clerk, Wilbur Smith, lives at the same place our pal Swope, here, did."

I said, "Let's get going," but we had to wait for the Homicide Squad. And Arnold had an argument with the radio car crew that beat them there; the radio crew took the newspaper talk about me being wanted for murder seriously.

MR. J. SWOPE had lived in a filthy hole, but he had been too smart to leave anything around that might have incriminated him. Even the labels were cut from his clothes. We did find what was left of a box of .45 shells and that was about all there was to show what Swope's business had been.

Arnold stared around and said, "What you going to do next, Shean?"

"What can I do? I'm afraid to go out on the street. The first cop that recognizes me will run me in, thanks to that screwy idea of yours."

He thought this was funny and said so. I went out with him to the police car and he said, "I got a good notion to throw Terwilliger in jail until this thing is over. That kid ain't safe."

"Under what bar table will you find him?"

"You want to go with me while I locate him?"

"I'm going down to the Martinez and talk to that clerk. He's working now."

Arnold said, "Get in and we'll both go."

We drove to the Martinez.

The clerk wasn't alone; we could see two women talking to him when Arnold coasted by the hotel entrance. He parked just beyond and we got out and went inside and both women turned at the noise.

I said, "Well, hello, Linda."

Linda Wilson looked as though she'd been crying. But a mad cry instead of a sad cry. She said, "Shean! I'm glad you're here. Make this man tell us what we want to know."

I looked at the other woman and saw she was blonde, gentle looking, and quite pretty. About twenty-two. Neither she or Linda belonged in a place like the Martinez, and I said,

"What's the idea, Linda?"

She waved at the girl friend, said, "Janet, this is Mr. Connell. Whom I told you of. Shean, this is Mrs. Janet Terwilliger."

Mrs. Terwilliger said, "Oh, Mr. Connell, won't you help me? I couldn't find my husband anywhere, and I think he's in this dreadful place. But this man won't tell us a thing."

Arnold growled, "Oh, he won't, won't he?" and reached over and caught Wilbur Smith by the coat lapels. With his left hand. He drew back his right, snapped, "O.K., guy! If you know what's good for you, you'll tell the lady what she wants to know."

Smith started his shimmy act. Shaking all over. He stammered, "Oh, sir! I really don't know a thing. A young man who resembles the description the lady gave me came in but went out. That was almost an hour ago."

"Who was he with?"

"I don't know. I really don't know."

"Who did he see?"

"He didn't see anybody. He asked for Mr. Swope and Mr. Swope wasn't here."

Sam, the bellboy, come down on the elevator then and I said, "Wait a minute, Arnie," and called Sam.

I described Terwilliger to him and he said he remembered him all right. And then I said, "Who did he see?"

"I let him off on the third floor. I brought him back a few minutes later."

"Who was with him?"

"Some older man. Looked like a big shot, like this guy you're talking about. I never seen him before. But say, Mr. Connell, he had a sort of black spot on his cheek, right by his nose."

Mrs. Terwilliger said, "That will be John Hempstead, Andy's partner. He has a mole on his cheek."

I said, "We're getting somewhere," and asked Arnold for the key we'd found on Swope. Then I asked the clerk:

"What's this look like?"

"A—a pass-key."

"Yours?"

"We—we have several of them here. It belongs to the hotel."

I said, "Now listen. You gave it to a guy named Swope, last night. He rode up in the elevator, while I was climbing the stairs. Isn't that right, Sam? Didn't you take a little thin guy up, while I climbed the stairs just before Dillon was killed?"

Sam opened his mouth and said this was right; but that he'd forgotten it during the excitement the night before.

The clerk said, "I—I should have told you. I know Mr. Swope quite well. He and I live in the same place on Tenth Avenue. We're very friendly. I know I shouldn't have given him the key, but we were friends."

I said to Arnold, "All right, that settles the Dillon kill. Swope did it with his little .45. When Ballistics check the slugs out of Dillon with that gun it will prove it. That robber cabby and I had a tail last night I didn't know of. Swope trailed me down here and got to Dillon first."

Mrs. Terwilliger and Linda had been listening to this as though they didn't understand it. Now Mrs. Terwilliger broke in with:

"But, Mr. Connell, where will I find Andy? I'm worried about him. Linda came to see me and I got hold of Andy at a bar, after Linda told me the dreadful things that were happening. He didn't wait at the bar for us, the way he said he would. The bartender said that he and another man had left, to go down here. We followed him. Now where is he?"

I said, "I'm going to ask you something personal. I want a fair answer, not colored by any personal prejudice. What kind of a woman was his first wife? Did you know her?"

"Yes, I knew Martha. Martha was an acquaintance of mine, before she divorced Andy."

"What's she like?"

"Well—well, I guess you could say she's weak. That's about all. I always liked Martha; I never could understand how she could fall in love with Laurence."

"You mean she fell in love with your husband's half-brother?"

This made her open her big blue eyes. She said, "Why, yes. Didn't Andy tell you?"

I said that Andy hadn't. She said that it had been almost a scandal; that Martha had divorced Andy, the brother with the money, to play around with Laurence, the brother with none. Arnold looked over at me then, said:

"I guess you got something there, Shean! There's motive and everything."

Mrs. Terwilliger said, "But I can tell you this. Martha wouldn't harm Andy for anything in the world."

"What about Laurence?"

She said she was sure Laurence wouldn't harm his brother, either, but she didn't sound convincing. I said to Linda: "Now you take Mrs. Terwilliger and go home."

She said she would and Arnold and I watched them leave. Then Arnold said to the clerk: "Come on, bud! You're going down to the station with me. Maybe you can think of something else."

I said, "I'm going out to Jerboe Road and talk to Hempstead."

"Maybe Terwilliger is there, too."

I said, "I doubt it. I've got a hunch that Hempstead will start doing his own work and not depend on hiring killers."

"Why Hempstead?"

"Why not. It's either Hempstead or this first wife or the half-brother who's after Terwilliger, isn't it? This wife here is too much worried about him to have him killed."

"Why not pick the half-brother? He needs the money. He probably thinks that Terwilliger is a heel for the way he treated the girl he's in love with?"

I said, "Why should he? He's got the girl."

Arnold shook his head and said he didn't know a thing about it and that none of it made sense. For that matter, it wasn't making too much sense to me. The only thing I was sure about was that the Mrs. Terwilliger I'd just met must be O.K. She was Linda's friend.

HEMPSTEAD HAD COMPANY when I got there. I paid off my cab, started to pass another one which was waiting, and a voice said:

"Hello, there, Mister! Did'ja make out all right last night?"

I saw it was the hacker that I'd ridden with the night before; the one with the trick meter in his cab. I said, "Yeah! I made out swell. Who you waiting for?"

"I bring out a gal and a guy. Just now. The guy tells me to wait."

"Know him?"

"The twist calls him Larry."

I said, "Thanks!" and started up to the house. I rang the bell and a pretty maid opened the door and told me she'd tell Mr. Hempstead I was there, but that she thought Mr. Hempstead was busy. She came back in a moment, led me into a room, and then Hempstead came in.

He stopped right by the door and looked me over and I saw the mole on his face that Mrs. Janet Terwilliger had described. He was short and blocky, about forty. He said, very briskly:

"Did I get that name right? Is it Mr. Connell?"

I said that was right.

"What is it you wish to see me about? You'll pardon me, but I have guests."

"I want to see them, too. It's about your partner. Is he with you?"

"Mr. Terwilliger stayed in town." He looked me over again, then his face brightened and he said: "Oh, I understand. You're the man Andy was telling me about. The detective."

"That's it. I'd like to see both you and Mr. Laurence Terwilliger and Mrs. Martha Terwilliger."

"What about?"

"For one thing, I want to know what you and Terwilliger were doing down at the Martinez tonight."

"I don't like your tone."

"Maybe you'll like the way the cops talk to you better?"

"I don't understand that. Why should the police talk to me?"

I put on my hat and said, "Oh, hell! We're not getting any place with this. You know what the idea is; you know that the police can ask you a lot of questions any time they want to do it."

He smiled then, said, "I'm afraid we're both inclined to be a little hasty with words, Mr. Connell. I apologize. I realize you're trying to help me."

"I'm trying to help Mr. Terwilliger."

"And you wish to see Mr. Laurence Terwilliger and Martha. Come with me."

He led me into another room and introduced me to the two. Laurence was maybe twenty-eight; a tall thin man. He was holding a drink, but not drinking it. Martha Terwilliger was a tall dark girl, with just a bit too much curve, though these were in the right places. She had very black eyes and wore her black hair in bangs. I don't like the type, but that wasn't really anything against the girl. We all sat down and I said:

"There's no reason I shouldn't tell you what I want. You all three of you know that Mr. Andrew Terwilliger hired me to investigate his death, don't you? Or is that news?"

Hempstead smiled and said he thought Mr. Andrew Terwilliger was a little excitable. I said, "Yeah, but somebody took three shots at him; that'll make anybody a bit nervous."

Martha said, "Andy was always inclined to dramatize himself. That accounts for this extended drinking bout of his; he told me he'd kill himself from drinking unless I went back to him."

I happened to look at Laurence Terwilliger then and saw the glance he gave her. Pure hate and disgust. But he said, "Are you going to do it?" in a civilized voice.

She laughed and said she hadn't decided what to do as yet and I saw Hempstead stare at her as if he were puzzled. She looked back at him, said, "I didn't tell you, John. Andy told me he has evidence against Janet and intends to divorce her. Of course you know Andy; you know you can't believe everything he says."

"I never found him that way," Hempstead said.

"I want to know one thing," I said. "What were you and Mr. Terwilliger doing down at the Martinez tonight, Mr. Hempstead?"

"I was with Andy and he wanted to see someone down there. I believe a man named Swope. The man Fat Dillon had called Andy and told him Swope knew something about the attempted murder. Andy wanted to investigate. Dillon had wanted money for this information. But we couldn't turn up Swope."

I said, "You might like to know that Swope was waiting for Terwilliger at Terwilliger's house, and died there. He was waiting to kill Terwilliger."

Hempstead said he didn't understand and I repeated it. Mrs. Terwilliger gave a little scream, then Laurence asked:

"What killed him?"

"A .45 slug. But before he died he talked to a policeman named Arnold for a while. If that means anything."

Then the maid came in and said, "There's someone on the phone for Mr. Connell. A lady, who insists he's here."

I'd been watching all three of them on the Swope death business and didn't see a thing. I went out in the hall and to the phone and Linda said:

"Shean! I just called the station to ask Mr. Arnold if he knew where I could find you, and he gave me this number. Something terrible has happened. Mr. Terwilliger is shot. Janet Terwilliger just called me and told me."

"Weren't you with her?"

"No. We separated when we left that terrible hotel. I went home. She just called a few minutes ago.

"Is Terwilliger dead?"

"Yes. He was in the back seat of his own car when they found him. She's all broken up about it."

I thanked her for calling and hung up the phone. And then went inside and said to the Martha woman: "Is there any way I can check on that statement you made about Mr. Terwilliger. About him going to divorce Janet and wanting to again marry you?"

Hempstead said, "Martha told me this same thing."

Martha said, "Check ahead. I don't know how you can, but it's *true*."

I said, "Well, I've taken up enough of your time. Thank you one and all for answering my questions. Good night."

Hempstead went to the door with me and I went out to the waiting cabby. I started to climb in and the cabby said, "Gee, chief, I'd like to ride you but I got these fares inside."

I said, "I don't give a damn about your fares inside. They'll ride in a police wagon. Get me to a telephone, quick."

I got Arnold, at the station, and he got in touch with the radio car in that district. I had to pass Hempstead's house, on the way back toward town, and the radio car was already in front.

LINDA WAS STILL up when the cab dropped me at her house. She said, "Oh, Shean! I feel terrible about this. Poor Janet was so broken up over it she could barely talk to me."

I said, "I want to talk to her. Can you call on her tonight and take me along? Tell her you want to know if you can be of help."

"But, Shean, she's in terrible shape!"

"She should be. She just shot her husband, I think. She ran out of hired killers and did the job herself."

"Shean, you're crazy!"

I borrowed Linda's phone and got Arnold again. I said, "Has that print man of yours found anything on the car you found Terwilliger in? Anything come out?"

"Some," Arnold said, and sounded puzzled. "A girl's prints, quite plain. We found two empty .25 automatic shells, too. Say, you were right about Swope killing Fat Dillon. But Dillon shot Lou Halper. Ballistics just reported that Halper was killed with Dillon's gun."

I said, "D'ya want to meet me at Mrs. Janet Terwilliger's house? She's the one that killed her old man."

"Are you sure?"

I said I was, but that the trick was going to be proving it. He said he'd meet me there, right away, and I said: "Not right away. Later."

"Shean! It's after three, now."

"What of it? We'll all be up."

He said I was crazy but that he'd play along and I hung up. Linda was standing there, all the time I talked to him, saying:

"Shean Connell! You're out of your mind."

I said, "Get your hat and coat on, honey, and let's go. I got a cab waiting."

The meter was four dollars and fifty cents even when we got outside, and the hacker saw me look at it and knocked the flag up and said, "Geez, chief, I forgot to get that clock checked today again. I always forget that, I swear I do."

I said, "You and that clock."

"I swear I'll do it tomorrow. But see, now it ain't registering."

He started to drive then, and I said to Linda, "I want a chance to look around this girl's bedroom."

"Why?"

"That's where she'd be most likely to hide the gun she used."

"She might have thrown it away."

I said, "Listen, hon, here's one thing that's a rule. A woman don't throw things like that away. She might give them away or sell them, but she don't throw them. Things like guns cost money."

We had an argument about this which neither of us won. And then I said, "But do me one thing. Watch her and tell me whether she's telling the truth about her dead husband. Will you do that?"

She said she would.

We got to Janet's apartment. Her maid opened the door and told us that Janet wasn't seeing anyone, but I said, "Oh, I'm sure that means everybody but Miss Wilson. You see, Mrs. Terwilliger just telephoned Miss Wilson."

That got us in, which was all I wanted. Mrs. Janet Terwilliger had a very swank five-room apartment. And as soon as I got in I didn't care about whether I searched the bedroom for the gun or not. There were pictures all over the place—one of Andy Terwilliger and at least a dozen of Laurence. Inscribed: *To my baby doll,* and little odds and ends like that. And Andy's picture looked as though it had been taken a couple of years before then and Laurence's looked new. I said to the maid:

"Where's the phone?" I got Arnold again. I said, "It's O.K., policeman. You can come up now and make your pinch and maybe we will get some sleep. It's air-tight, now. I've even got the motive."

LINDA RODE DOWN to jail with Janet, still not believing it. But about the time they took her prints and matched them with those found where Terwilliger had been killed, and about the time the matron started searching her, she broke.

Arnold found the gun hidden under a pile of silk things in a dresser drawer, and the shells found fitted the gun. All this took time, though, and it was seven o'clock before Linda and Arnold and I got away from the station and got breakfast.

Then Linda said, "But I don't see how you knew Janet did it."

Arnold grinned his slow way and said, "It had to be one of the four, Miss Wilson. All Shean had to do was find out which one it was."

I said, "It wasn't too hard, hon. She told me, down at the Martinez when I first met her, that Laurence was in love with Martha. He wasn't. She said Martha was weak, easily led. She wasn't. She was lying to throw suspicion on Martha. That's all. She had this affair with her husband's half-brother and Terwilliger must have been getting wise to it. He'd have divorced her and cut off that policy, so she hired him killed. Hired Swope to do it. Lou Halper got suspicious of Dillon when he investigated the attempted murder of Terwilliger. It seems reasonable to believe that Halper went after Dillon and that Dillon killed him. He probably hid the body in that closet, figuring to take it away later. But Swope killed him before he could do it."

Arnold said, "That's something I don't get. Why should Swope kill Dillon?"

"Swope followed me down there. He must have been watching Terwilliger and seen him talk to me. So he must have figured I'd talk to Dillon and that maybe Dillon knew Swope was hired for the kill. He wanted to get Dillon before Dillon talked to me. That's the logical answer; Dillon found that Janet had hired Swope to get her old man out of the way, and Dillon figured he could shake Swope down. That would explain him being close to the scene of the first shooting. Hanging around so he could do a little blackmail later on. Right away he tried to sell Terwilliger information about Swope. Working both ends against the middle. But Swope killed him before he talked."

Linda mourned, "And to think she killed her husband herself. She seemed such a nice girl, too."

"Nice people are mixed up in murders all the time, honey. Believe it or not. She just got tired waiting for her hired killer to do the job and did it herself."

We got through breakfast and started out, Arnold going back to the station and Linda and I heading for home. And just about half a block down the street from the station somebody gripped my arm and said:

"All right, Connell! Come quietly." I turned and there was a policeman.

I asked him what he wanted me for and he said, "Murder. The want's out for you. Killing Dillon and Halper."

"They'll probably put me in and throw the key away. The other Mrs. Terwilliger is going to sue me for false arrest, you know. Also Laurence. The two damn fools don't realize I had to have them held as material witnesses."

"I'll go along, too," Linda said. "I suppose this is just the start of a habit. I suppose that if I do marry you I'll do most of my housekeeping in a jail."

I said, "Well, I'll give you your same argument. You meet nice people there. You've even got friends there, hon. Girl friend first, and now boy friend."

One Good Turn

A blonde's jewels lead Shean Connell into gun talk

I'D JUST COME out of my hotel and was standing in front of it trying to make up my mind. It was a problem. It was lunch time and I was about half hungry and I could go down to the corner and eat a sandwich and drink a glass of beer, or I could go back inside and into the bar, take a real drink, and then eat a regular meal. The pros and cons were whirling around when I looked up and saw a good-looking girl heading out past me from the lobby.

She was young and blonde and nice looking and she wore a worried look. She stood beside me, acting as undecided as I was, and for a moment I got the idea she was trying for a pick-up.

But she didn't have the speculative look a girl on the make usually has, so I decided I'd made a bad guess.

For that matter, I wasn't greatly interested. Making plays for strange girls on the street is usually disappointing. Either you don't get the girl, which is a let down, or you get her and she proves out a dud.

So we both just stood there, looking each other over casually and neither making a move to do anything about it. I decided on the real drink and a steak, and I turned back to the hotel and into the bar. I ordered straight rye, then looked around and saw the same girl come up to the bar alongside me. She said to Mike, the barman on shift at that end:

"Tom Collins."

Mike turned and reached for the gin bottle, and the girl said to me: "Take this quick! I'll call you about it."

She handed me a package about as big as a match-box. When
somebody holds out something to take you, usually take it and
I did. But it was a bit more than startling and all I could think
of to say was:

"Hunh?"

She'd just whispered the first. Now she said, right out loud:
"I *beg* your pardon."

Mike had turned around with the Tom Collins for her and
half a grin for me. She took her glass and slid down the bar
until she was about ten feet from me and I got the idea then.
I put the package in my pocket, poured myself another drink,
and said to Mike, making it loud enough for her to hear:

"I'm going down to Harry's Chop House and get a bite to

eat. I'm going to stay in the room the rest of the day and catch up on my rest."

The girl looked around at me with a who-the-hell-cares look and finished her drink. She left the bar and Mike said:

"These babes'll really fool a man. I don't blame you for making a pass. She *looked* playful."

I said, "She probably plays different games than I do. Me, I like post-office but not ring-around-the-rosy."

He looked very wise and said: "They all play. But sometimes they only play with Mr. Right."

I agreed with the first part and paid for my drinks and then kept my word and went down to Harry's and ate a steak. And then back to my room to see what the little stranger had left with me.

The little package was wrapped as though it had been done in a hurry. Just flimsy paper around a pill box. The pill box was lettered:

Laird's Pharmacy
No. 118396—Buell
As Directed
Conover.
10-4-37.

Just like the top of any drugstore pillbox, but the inside looked as though the box should have been from a jewelry store instead of drugstore. There were four rings in it. Two diamond, one ruby, and one emerald. The two diamond rings would weigh four carats apiece. The ruby was as big and the emerald was a dinner ring and even bigger.

All four were mounted in platinum and all of them looked like good stones, and while I'm no jewel expert I thought the collection would probably bring around twenty thousand or up. Even at a fire sale. I know enough about gems to understand the bigger the stone is the more it's worth in proportion; a two-carat stone would be worth more than twice as much as a carat stone of the same grade. They go up the scale like that in value. So I didn't think twenty thousand would be stretching it.

It made a puzzle. I tried to think why a pretty blonde should pass me anything like that and finally decided I had the answer. About then the phone rang and a girl's voice said:

"Mr. Connell? Mr. Shean Connell?"

I said, "Speaking."

She said, "You know who *I* am."

"I'm sorry," I told her.

"You know—at the bar."

"Oh, yes. I'd almost forgotten."

"I want to see you."

"Come on up."

"I'm being followed."

"Who's tagging you?"

"I don't know. It's been different men."

I laughed then and said, "Sure. All of them are cops."

"Why do you say that?"

"Why girlie-girlie me?" I said. "This stuff you gave me is hot and you're burning up with it. I'm going to turn it over to the law and clear myself and I'm going to do it quick. You might as well let your tag catch up with you; it's just a matter of time, anyway, before they do."

I meant this and she must have decided from my voice that I did. She said, "Oh my God! Don't! Don't! Let me see you and explain."

"I'm no go-between on any stolen ice. Not any."

Then she said, "I know that. That's why I gave them to you. Linda and I were talking and she thought I should do it."

I said, "Linda?"

She said, "Linda Wilson."

That stopped me and upset my stolen jewel theory. Linda Wilson and I had been playing around together for some little time. Linda was the girl friend and nice people in spite of it. I had the notion that any friend of hers would be nice people too, and that at least they'd have a story it wouldn't do any harm to hear. So I said:

"O.K. Go down to Market and watch for some big store

that's having a sale. Like the Emporium or Hale's. Go in and mill around with the crowd and don't do a half-way job of it. Then duck out fast and catch a hack in a hurry. Wait until you're sure you're not being followed by another Cab and then go to the Dexter Hotel and register under the name of Mary Gillis. This ought to lose your tag and if it don't it still won't make a hell of a lot of never minds. Get the picture?"

She said she understood, but what would happen if she didn't manage to lose her shadow? I told her to never mind about that but to just do the best she could and I hung up the phone to stop any argument.

I WENT DOWNSTAIRS, caught a cab to the Central Station, and wandered into the Robbery Detail, as though I was just killing time.

George Sanders was there and I'd known him for a long time. But we had to go through an act before I could find out a thing. First, he ribbed me about being a shamus, which according to him is even lower than a piano player in the scheme of things. I'd played piano for years before starting an agency. I ribbed back about him working for the city, claiming this was petty larceny in its cheapest form. After we got through these preliminaries I dug around and asked a few questions about crime in general and about the jewel robbery end of it in particular and found out he didn't know a thing about four big rings being missing from some tax-payer.

I bought him a couple of beers then, so he wouldn't think I was after anything important, and then headed for the Dexter and waited in the lobby to see what I could see.

It timed out very well. About twenty minutes after I was

there the blonde came in. She hurried by me, not seeing me, and went right to the desk.

Right after her came Jake Abrams.

Jake saw me but pretended he didn't. He started by and I looked up, pretended to notice him for the first time, and stood. I said:

"Why hello, Jake! What in hell are you doing here?"

"Hi, Shean," he said. "I didn't see you."

He kept looking over at the desk where the blonde was registering. He looked hot and bothered and as though I was the last man in the world he wanted to see. I said:

"Long time no see. Come on in to the bar and I'll buy a drink."

He said: "I'm—uh—" and kept looking after the blonde, who was now following a boy toward the elevator bank.

"Working?" I asked.

"Oh, no. Just looking for a friend." The elevator door blanked the blonde from sight and Jake shook his head and turned and said, "I'm supposed to meet this guy right here. If it wasn't for that, I'd take that drink. I don't want to miss this guy."

I said, "Guy, hell. Gal, you mean."

"It's a guy, Shean."

"Like hell. Just like always. You're in there pitching every second."

He grinned as though I was right and I decided he was satisfied to have me think he had a date with some tart. I *knew* he was on business because he'd have gone for the drink if he hadn't been working.

I'd always liked Jake. I stalled him along for a while longer, long enough for the girl to get upstairs and settled in her room, and then I headed for the washroom and gave the bell captain the eye while I was passing him. He followed me in and I told him a friend of mine and I were waiting for the same girl and that I wanted to see her first. I gave him a dollar and told him to find what room Mary Gillis had and to soft pedal the finding out.

He came back and told me 518. I went back through the lobby, waving at Jake, where he was sitting and watching the elevators, and went around to the freight elevator and paid the porter another dollar for a ride to the fifth on it.

It was that easy, and I patted myself on the back for out-smarting Jake Abrams.

Like a fool.

I hunted for 518, found it and knocked on the door. The blonde opened it and let me in, peeking up and down the hall as though she was chiseling and didn't want the head man to find it out. She almost whispered:

"I think I'm still being followed."

I said, "I know you are. By a tall dark man."

She stared at me as though I'd been looking in crystal. I made it even better by telling her: "His name is Jake Abrams and he's the best man Alliance, Inc., has on the payroll."

"Do you know him?"

"Sure."

"Are you sure he works for this detective agency?" she asked, looking as though she'd heard good news.

I said, "Yeah. It's a sort of private insurance company that takes over some business from the big line companies."

She said: "Oh!" and looked as if I'd smacked her in the face. I explained it a bit more with:

"It's like this. Suppose an insurance company takes out a blanket policy on the contents of a house or store. If there's jewelry or furs or something that's compact and valuable and easily stolen, they can farm out that part of the business. The Alliance people specialize in these risks. I don't imagine it's a common thing but it must happen once in a while because the Alliance people seem to be getting along and paying dividends. Jake Abrams is their star man. Understand it now?"

She said she did.

I said: "All right. Now who are you and what's the yarn?"

"I'm Ann Willard—Mrs. Hugh Willard. The rings are mine. They were stolen and then returned."

I got another idea then. It made sense, after what I'd figured and after seeing Jake Abrams. I said, "You mean they were returned after the insurance company had paid off. Is that it?"

"Yes."

"Listen, Mrs. Willard," I said. "That's too raw to get by in this day and age. That gag was old when pop was in knee pants. That gag's been worked ever since there were insurance companies and they all know it. You pretend something insured is stolen and they pay off. Nuts! Here's your stuff and you battle it out with Abrams. If you're nice about it, they may let you off without making charges. I'd take a bet either way on it."

I tossed her the pill-box of jewels and started for the door and she ducked around in front of me and stood in front of it with her arms spread wide. I'd have to walk either over, or through her to get out of the room. She cried out:

"Please! Please, Mr. Connell! Hear the rest. Let me tell you."

I said: "O.K.," thinking I might as well listen as long as I was blocked off from the door. But I didn't expect to hear any new angles on a racket as old as that one was. She said, almost crying:

"Please! I didn't do what you're thinking. They were really stolen."

"Who stole them?"

She shook her head and said she didn't know and I said, "The only thing you can do is give the insurance company back their money and tell them what's happened. That's your only out. That and prayer. If you're nice they may pass the thing, as I say."

She said, "I can't do that. The insurance money's been stolen, too."

"My God!" I said. "You must live in a den of thieves."

She shook her head again, as though she didn't understand it herself, and said, "I cashed the check the insurance company gave me and took the money home. I was going to deposit it in my own bank the next morning. It was taken that night."

"Why didn't you just deposit the check?"

"I should have, I know. I just didn't think. It was twenty-two thousand, eight hundred and forty dollars."

"Do you expect me to believe this yarn of yours?" I asked.

"I hope you will."

"Then you'd better put in what you've left out. And give me credit for a little brains. That bit about taking the check to a bank and then cashing it and then bringing the dough home with you with the idea of depositing it in your own bank in the morning doesn't make sense. A ten-year-old kid wouldn't do a fool thing like that. I *can* believe the stones were lifted. That's possible. I *can* believe the dough the insurance company gave you was lifted. I *can't* believe this other. Why take the check to a strange bank in the first place? Why take the dough home?

Did you just want to look at it? Stay on your merry-go-round, sister, but stay on it by yourself."

I put out my hand to push her to the side so I could get out, but she caught my hand and cried, "I can't tell you why I took the money home. I can't. I just can't!"

She was crying to beat the band and holding to my hand as if she was drowning and going under for the third time. I said, "Does it have anything to do with you stealing your own rings?"

I thought I'd make her mad and snap her out of the crying that way but it didn't work out. She kept on with my hand and said, "I swear I didn't do that. I didn't know I needed any money until a month after the rings were stolen. Please, please believe me."

I didn't believe her exactly, but in a funny sort of way I did. I knew I shouldn't; knew it must be a framed theft because of the jewels being returned, but I half-way believed her in spite of it, I let her hold my hand and said:

"Well, go on."

"That's all. The money was taken the night I took it home. About a week later I found the rings in our mail-box. They were wrapped the same way they were when I gave them to you. I didn't know what to do with them and Linda said I should talk to you. She told me where you lived and I've seen her pictures of you. I saw that man following me when I was headed for your hotel. I saw you in the lobby and I felt suddenly I had to get rid of them."

I said, "Let's go to your house now. I want to talk with your help and I want to see where this money was taken from. And where you kept these rings."

She handed me back the loot and we started out, leaving the hotel by the freight elevator.

THE WILLARDS HAD a nice place out Pacific Avenue way and just off it; far enough out to be in a decent neighborhood and not so far as the trick palaces some people built who should have known better. Maybe ten, maybe twelve rooms, and set far enough back from the street so they wouldn't have been bothered by people going by looking in at them. I paid the cabby and we went up on the porch and while she was fumbling around in her purse for a key the door opened and a man said:

"Why, Ann! I didn't know you planned on being out today."

Ann blushed and said, "Hugh, this is Mr. Connell. He's a friend of Linda Wilson's. Mr. Connell, my husband."

Hugh said, "Oh, yes!" as though he knew and didn't approve, and then to his wife: "I just this minute came in. Just this minute." He explained even further to me: "I'm usually at my office at two in the afternoon."

Mrs. Willard led the way inside and said, "Shall we talk in here? Hugh didn't know I was going to talk to you today. To be frank, he doesn't quite approve."

She opened the door at the right-hand side of the hall and then screamed at the top of her voice and started to fall. Willard stood there, like a big stupid, but I caught her in time to keep her from knocking what brains she had out against the floor and eased her down. I said to him:

"Get water!" and then looked past her to see what had caused the excitement.

I saw it.

A man was draped over the end of a davenport that stood in the center of the room. The light was on and I could see the side of his head and it was covered with blood. Willard didn't go after the water but stared inside as I did, and he said, in a startled voice:

"That's blood!"

"Sure," I said. "Get some water quick. I'll look after this."

I left Ann Willard on the floor and went in the room. I could see the man was dead before I got within ten feet of him. There was a piece of skull knocked in so deep you could see it through his hair. I got to the side, so that I could see the other side of his face, and then decided somebody had maybe done the world a favor. At least, in a way.

It was Barney Ransom, who was half of Barnett and Ransom, Private Investigations. Their specialty was framing people and acting as go-betweens between blackmailers and victims and they did a little high-class fence business on the side. Two nice boys, who were always just on the edge of losing their license but always wiggled clear.

But after all, this was murder and that's carrying things to extremes, even with a heel like Ransom.

Willard said from right behind me: "I'll call the police!"

I turned around and said, "If you don't get that water and get it right now they'll need an ambulance as well as a morgue wagon. The ambulance for you."

He left on that one. He was slick and dapper, one of the smooth sort of men that make me glad I'm not. I went to Barney and looked inside what pockets I could, without moving him, and didn't find a thing except that somebody had the same idea before me. Some of the pockets were turned inside out. Willard came back with a glass of water and I took it and said:

"Now call the cops. The number of the Central Station is at

the top of the phone book and when you get the station you ask for Homicide. When you get Homicide, ask for Sergeant Keene. Tell him the address and tell him I'm here and that a dead man is here. Understand that?"

He said, "I'm not a fool."

I said, "There are two sides to every argument."

He gave me a dirty look and stepped over his wife as though she was a rug. I wet my handkerchief and held it on her forehead and by and by she shuddered and mumbled:

"I thought I saw—" and then opened her eyes.

I said, "Now keep your nerve. You saw it."

That snapped her out of it. She opened her mouth to scream again and I slapped her across the cheek and said, "None of that. Mind me."

She shook her head, like a thoroughbred, and said, "I'm all right. It startled me. I'm nervous at all times; more so these past days."

"Did you know a man named Barney Ransom?"

"No."

"Chuck Barnett?"

"No, I've never heard either of the names."

I said, "You'll hear 'em again. Often."

I helped her to her feet and Willard came back and said: "Your friend says he is on his way." He made "friend" stand out and I got the idea. Keene is a tough cop and I judged Willard got that idea, even over the phone.

I closed the door into the murder room and we stood there in the hall and waited for the police. The first group came on the district dolly car and the two boys in the crew came in and I told them what was in the other room. They told me they'd got the flash from the station and then went in and took a look.

The next was a fast wagon from the station, with Keene and two other Homicide men. One named Kitt and the other Mahlon. Of course Kitt is called Kitty by his friends, but *only* by them because he weighs two hundred and forty pounds and is a tough egg. Mahlon is little and round and rosy, with a bay window that's the first thing you notice when you meet him. Mahlon is a good man; Kitt is a heel.

Sergeant Keene came in with the troupe and said, "Always, Shean, where you go we find bodies."

I didn't say anything back. Kitt gave me a dirty grin and said, "Too damned handy with a gun and with your lip. That's the matter with you, Connell."

I said, "O.K., Kitty, O.K. This guy's head was bashed in. It was done before I got here. I can prove it. Does that straighten it out for you?"

He said, "*We* don't know that's straight."

Keene said, "Now you guys don't start that wrangling around; There's no need and no sense in it."

I introduced him to Willard and Mrs. Willard and then showed the three of them the corpse. Keene looked Ransom over and made sure he was dead, and then said to Mahlon:

"Call the M.E., the print man, and the photographer. They'll be in a pinochle game if they ain't playing hearts. Tell 'em to get out here." Then he asked us all in general:

"Who found him?"

Willard told him, "We all did. Mr. Connell just arrived, with Mrs. Willard—two seconds after I did—and we started in the room to have a talk. He—it was here like this."

Keene put his hands on his hips and spread his feet apart.

He rocked back and forth, heel and toe, and said:

"And, of course, that was the first time any of you ever *did* see him?"

I said, "Now Keene! You know damn well I knew Barney Ransom. Just the same as I know Chuck Barnett, his partner."

Both the Willards swore they'd never met Ransom.

We stalled around until the print man and the rest of the crew came along, and then the M.E. made his look and said Ransom had been dead since about twelve noon. That was approximate, of course. Sometime between eleven and twelve-thirty for sure.

I said, "That lets me out of the picture, if I ever was in it." This was for Kitt's benefit, because he'd been pinning a you're-the-one-that-did-it look on me ever since he'd been in the place. "Check this if you want. At that time, or between that time, I was at Harry's Chop House. I eat there all the time and they know me. Look it up."

Kitt looked as though it wasn't worth the effort. I said, "Go ahead and check it. I talked to Harry himself, he stopped by my booth. Call him up. I've got trouble enough without having the law think I'm in the murder racket. And Mrs. Willard was with me almost immediately afterwards."

Kitt went to the phone and called Harry's, which is what I wanted. If he'd waited until afterwards it would have given him a chance to say I'd fixed up the alibi.

Then it was Willard's turn. He had Keene call his office and some girl there said that Mr. Willard had just left and would probably be home by now. There was no particular reason to figure Willard as the killer anyway, outside of the deed happening in his house, so Keene pretended to be satisfied with this.

But he said:

"Now Connell is alibied and Mrs. Willard is alibied because she was with him. You're alibied by your office. But that don't get away from the fact that there's a dead man here and the man was murdered. The man was no good on earth, I'll admit that, but murder's murder. If I find a hole in one of these three perfect alibis, you can guess what I'm going to do about it."

We all said we had an idea of what he'd do.

The dead wagon took Ransom away, after the photographer had smoked the place up with flash-light powder, and then we all went in another room and Keene spent the next two hours asking questions and not learning a thing. We were all careful not to mention the jewelry.

He finally got ready to leave and then said to me: "You want to ride back with me, Shean?"

I said, "Hell, no. I came out to talk with Mr. and Mrs. Willard and haven't had the chance. I'll stick for a while."

Willard said, "My wife is in no condition to talk. This shock and all. Suppose we postpone it."

I looked at her and saw she was staring at him as though he was the candy kid and made the world, so I took him to the side and said:

"It's O.K. by me. It's you I want to talk with, anyway."

He said, "Suppose we say in my office at ten," and gave me an address on Market, and I told him it was a date and rode back to town with Keene.

SERGEANT KEENE DROPPED me at my hotel about 5:30 and I sailed in and over to desk to see if I had any mail. Jake Abrams said, right over my shoulder:

"What kind of a yarn did she have? Find out where the stuff was, did you? Did she keep it or have you got it?"

I said, "Who? What yarn? What stuff?" thinking, all the time, what a fool I was to think I'd been putting anything over on Jake.

He said, "I mean Mrs. Willard. Mary Gillis, I guess you'd call her. That bellboy would sell his soul for another buck—from you or me."

After me thinking I'd pulled a smartie with the freight elevator gag! I said, "You win!" and gave him the package with the four rings. It wasn't mine and it wasn't Mrs. Willard's since she'd been paid for it. It was the insurance company's and Jake represented them.

I said: "I'll buy you that drink now, Jake. You've got what you're after."

He said, "Sure, Shean. I'll buy one myself; I'm on expense money and the company ought to stand for it; they're getting their property back, aren't they?"

We went in the bar and sat down and I told him the story, leaving nothing out. When I came to the girl's argument about not stealing her own rings he grinned and said:

"And at your age, you believe. Shean! How does Santa make it down these narrow flues?"

He told me his company got a tip and he'd been assigned to it. Some man called in and said the steal had been a phony. Abrams said the minute he'd started to tag around after Mrs. Willard she'd acted the same. I said:

"That's well and good. You've got the ice and I suppose you've got a fraud case against her if you want to go ahead with it. She tells me she hasn't got the money she got from your company, so I don't see how you're going to get that back."

Abrams grinned and said, "That's up to the company's lawyers, not to me. I just do my work and let the others worry about theirs."

"It's past that with me, Jake. Now Barney Ransom is murdered and I was working for this woman while he was. She and her husband are mixed in that some way, just how I don't know. It's only reasonable to suppose that this ice is mixed in the deal as well."

"I can see that," Abrams said.

We talked it over, making no more sense out of it, until finally he said, "I've got to be getting home. My car's outside."

I walked outside with him. Side by side we went. He had a sedan and had left it locked and he was bending over the door, fitting a key into the lock and I was standing by him.

I didn't hear a sound. I was looking down at him as he swung the door open, and I just saw a hand and arm from behind us flash down against Abram's head. The hand held a sap and I could hear the *thwacking* sound the sap made against Abrams' head.

I started to turn and this probably saved me from the full effect of the smack I got right then. It caught me about half on the cheek, instead of landing full on my head.

At that, it did the business. I wasn't out but I was paralyzed. I could see Abrams face go down into the running-board of his car, and I couldn't prevent falling against it, almost above him.

Somebody caught me and I could hear a voice say, "Get the rear door open, Monk. Quick."

At the same time a hand caught me by the shoulder and steadied me, so that I didn't fall quite all the way down. The blow had dazed me and I couldn't straighten my head—just kept staring down at Abrams, all crumpled there, and I saw him yanked back away from the car, although I couldn't see who had done this. The hand on my shoulder pulled me away from the car, someone opened the back door, and then the hand gave me a push into the car.

I fell in. Across the floor. The sudden move did what the blow hadn't quite accomplished, and I went out like a light.

I WAS SITTING on the back seat when I came back to life, propped against the back just like I belonged there and was there because I'd wanted to be. The man sitting by me was a quiet look-ing sort of person, brown-haired, brown-eyed, and the same sort of complexion. He looked as though he'd spent a lot of time on the golf links. He was short and wide and I judged him around my own weight, close to a hundred and ninety. I said:

"What's the idea, mister?"

He said, "Never mind, Connell. Just keep quiet about it." And then nudged me with the gun he was holding against me.

He'd sort of drawled his words out in a soft and pleasant voice, but he sounded as though he meant what he said. We rode on, came to where a new Ford sedan was parked, and he drawled at me:

"We change cars here. This is ours. No reason in taking chances on a stolen car rap."

He sounded as if the whole thing was just run of the mill stuff to him, and the attitude was one I didn't like. Being kidnaped didn't fit any picture I could see, any more than the stolen jewelry and the dead Barney Ransom did. We changed into the Ford and the man who had been driving us said:

"He's no trouble at all. Is he, Chas?"

Chas said, "Dummy up. We're not through yet. That'll be the time to talk."

The other giggled, very girlishly, and said: "All the time ribbing. Ribbing all the time."

Chas said, in his nice quiet drawling way: "Shut your —— mouth, Monk, and keep it shut. I'm sick of it and you both."

The guy called Monk stopped his giggle and didn't lose any time at it. He said, very apologetically:

"Sure, Chas."

He wheeled away from the curb and down the street, as though he knew just where he was going, and we went a couple of blocks without anyone saying a word. Then I said:

"What was the idea in sapping Abrams, if it was me you were after? How was he in this?"

Chas said, "Was his name Abrams? We didn't want him along and so we left him where he landed."

The driver said, "Yeah! You're all we need," and laughed as if this was funny.

"Shut up," Chas said again.

The driver had a long, freckled, sandy-colored neck and he was wearing a shirt with a low collar attached so that I got the full benefit of the neck. He had ears that stood out straight from his head and they were so big I'll bet he could have flapped them twice and flown like a bird. I looked him over while we went on a few more blocks and decided I'd know him if I ever saw him again, even from this back view. Finally the driver said:

"You don't need to get sore at me, Chas. I was just ribbing, sort of."

I looked sidewise at Chas and saw his lips tighten and the muscles along his jaw harden. I also got a fair look at his eyes and understood what was the matter with him; why he'd taken the unnecessary smack at Jake Abrams and why he was so tough with his partner in crime. He was high; so high his eyes looked out of focus. The dope he had in him hadn't affected his voice or movements, but it had brought out every bit of meanness in his make-up. He was sitting there trying to work himself into a rage, and the damned fool driving the car didn't have brains enough to realize it. My only out was to start something.

I thought this over and decided right then was as good a time as any to make the move. He had a gun in his left hand, the hand on the far side from me, and his right hand was still out in front of him and just above his legs. I threw myself across him, so that it forced the loose arm down between his knees. It kept this arm out of action. I got his other wrist with one hand and the gun with the other, and I caught the gun by the cylinder, so that he couldn't pull the trigger if he wanted to do it. A revolver can't shoot if the cylinder is held like this and I depended on this fact; that is, it won't shoot unless it happens to be fully cocked, which this gun wasn't. I twisted my hands in opposite directions, so that his finger was caught in the trigger guard, and after a bit of this kind of pressure he said:

"I quit." And he hadn't even lost his easy drawl!

I didn't blame him for quitting. If he didn't quit he'd have had a busted finger and I'd have had the gun just the same. I slid back into my corner and turned the gun on him, and he didn't change his expression at all. I said:

"Have you got a record?"

He shrugged his shoulders and rubbed his sore finger and said, "You can find that out. We can all go up to the station and see whether I have or not."

It was smart. He hadn't taken my gun from me and it would have looked silly, driving up to the station in his car and holding his own gun on him; There wasn't a way in the world to prove he'd smacked Abrams; all he had to do was deny it. How could I prove it? If we went to the station and he happened to be on the wanted list it would be fine. If he wasn't on the list I'd have been kidded out of town. It was an even bet, whether to go or not, and I couldn't make up my mind about which way to go on it. I said to the driver:

"All right, Bat Ears. Into the curb."

I wasn't giving the driver credit for being as smart as he was. Of course he'd heard the rumpus and he knew the apple cart was tipped over but it had only taken a minute and he'd been too busy with the car to interfere with me. Now he did just exactly what I'd told him to do; went into the curb.

He went first class, too, when he did. He just swung on the wheel, put his arms up over his face to save himself from the glass, and shoved his foot flat down to the floor, putting the motor wide open.

We were probably going about thirty when we hit and we smacked into the back of a car that was just pulling away from the curb. We hit hard enough to knock me from the seat to the floor. The fall tangled me some but I managed to keep the gun trained on Chas, but I don't think it made any difference because he didn't seem to make any attempt at getting away. I got back on the seat, put the gun I'd taken away from him in my pocket, but so it still covered him, and said:

"Get out."

He reached to the side and opened the door without looking at it and started to back out, still watching me. And then, all of a sudden, he went back and out of the car as though a rope was tied on him.

I followed him out and then felt sorry for him.

A big fat woman had him by the back of the collar with one hand and by the slack of his coat in back with the other. She'd yanked him out and was shaking him like she could have shaken a rag doll. And this with him weighing as much as I do. She was saying:

"See! See! See what you done to my fender? See!"

And with every "see" she bounced him up and down on the pavement.

I got a flash of Bat Ears taking off through the crowd that had already gathered and then looked over and saw the big gal's car had a smashed rear fender and that our Ford had a blown front tire and a smashed headlight. I turned back to the action in time to hear the fat girl say:

"You'll pay for this. It's your fault."

I moved in closer and winked, very dirtily, at Chas, and said, "That's right, lady! It's his car and he's stuck, even if he wasn't driving."

She turned and glared at me. Then she decided I was on her side and cried out:

"He just ran into me on purpose."

"I saw the whole thing," I said. "I'll swear he did that. It was deliberate."

This was the first time that Chas had changed expression since I'd met him. She was still bouncing him up and down and he was high enough to let her. It didn't look as though he'd even been trying to get away and he'd kept that sort of screwy look on his pan all through it. But now he turned his head and snarled at me:

"You dummy up!"

I said, "You can't scare me. I saw the whole thing. I'll swear you ran into the lady."

I winked at him again and he looked as though he'd have bitten me if the big gal had turned him loose. A traffic cop came bustling through the crowd and she finally let Chas go and said to the cop:

"He ran into me, Officer. On purpose, he ran into me. This man saw it all." She pointed at me and the cop looked and waved and said:

"Hi, Connell."

He was stationed near my hotel and I happened to know him. The cop looked at Chas and said, "This your car?"

The big girl said, "It certainly is. He was riding in back, but he has to pay for the damages, just the same."

The cop looked Chas over and asked him if he'd been drinking. Chas said he hadn't. I could have told the cop the same answer—a junk-head doesn't often go for liquor and Chas was higher than a kite. The cop sniffed a bit and said, very regretfully:

"I guess you haven't. Let me see your driver's license."

"I wasn't driving," Chas told him.

"I didn't ask you that. I said 'let's see your driving license.' Are you going to show me that license or are you going to tell me you haven't got one?"

Chas showed his license. The cop looked at it and compared

it with the registration slip on the car's steering wheel. Then he said:

"It's your car, all right. Now just what is the yarn?"

I didn't wait to hear whether Chas told him the truth or not. I'd been peeking over the cop's shoulder and I saw the license read Charles Moody, 2217 Grenoble St. That was all I wanted. I picked a cab that had stopped because of the excitement, and said:

"Twenty-two-hundred block on Grenoble. I'm in a hurry."

The only reason I'd taken the big girl's side of the argument had been to make sure Chas had to show who he was and where he lived. I'd found it out and I couldn't see any sense in hanging around. I wanted to be waiting for Chas when he got home and outside of a bad tire his car wasn't hurt and I didn't have too much time.

THE TWENTY-TWO HUNDRED block on Grenoble was full of "Rooms for Rent" places. I went up to 2217 and a lady opened the door and I said in my best manner:

"I'm looking for a room."

She beamed at me and said, "I have a very nice room. Upstairs." She didn't give me a chance to say a word, just went into a sales talk about what a nice place and what a nice room and how some of her roomers just hated to leave her when they went, and finally I broke in and said:

"O.K., lady. I'll take it."

"But don't you want to see it?"

I saw a cab coming down the street and said, "Yes, please," trying to get inside and out of sight. We did, just as the cab pulled up in front. The lady said:

"I'll get the key. Just a moment," and left me standing in the hall, and the front door opened and Bat Ears walked in and saw me.

He said: "Huh!" just as though somebody had poked him in the tummy. Which I did, without delay, with the gun I'd taken away from Chas.

I said, "Keep that trap of yours closed or you'll take it right here."

He stood there and I stood there, both of us holding the pose, and then the landlady came back. In the dark hall she couldn't see the gun.

She said, "Oh! Do you know Mr. Thomas?"

I said, "Sure. A long time. We were in a car wreck together once."

Thomas stuck his long neck even farther up out of his collar and swallowed. His Adam's apple went up and down a couple of times and he started to say something. I leaned on the gun and he changed his mind. The landlady beamed on us both and said:

"Now isn't that nice! Your room will be right across the hall from his. Come, I'll show you."

She turned toward the stairs and I said, "Mr. Thomas can show me. Can't you, Tommy?"

He made a noise that could have meant yes or practically anything else and I took the key from her with my free hand and we went upstairs. We left her at the bottom of them, smiling up at us. We got to the top and I said:

"We'll go to your room. You've got some talking to do."

He bobbed his head and opened a door and we went in. I shook him down, not finding a gun, then sat him down in a chair and said:

"What's this all about?"

He asked, "You mean about us guys picking you up like that?"

I said, "You dope! Spit it out."

He didn't hold back. He said, "Me and Chas was walking down the street and we meet a guy we know and he asks us do we want to make a dime and we say yes. That was just a minute before we see you in the bar. The guy points you out and you come outside and Chas takes you. That's all I know."

"Who was this guy?"

"Chuck Barnett. He's a looker-inner."

This didn't clear things much. Barnett was Ransom's partner, and even with Ransom dead and in such a way I was mixed with it, I couldn't see any kidnaping reason. Barnett could easily enough find out my connection with Ransom's death was only through my client; that Ransom had been found in her house. I said:

"What were you supposed to do with me?"

"Just keep you away for four or five days. That's all. We was going to take you—"

I said, "Skip it. Now, listen. I've got friends on the force and I'm going to do this. As long as you and Chas stay right at this place, I'm going to let you. If you start to take a powder you won't get to the end of the block."

"You can't make a cry," he said. "You can't prove we did a thing."

I said, "Shut up. Did I say I wanted to prove anything? Do you want to go to the station and have the boys work you over while they check you up? I've got friends there; you haven't."

He said, "I get it. I'll stay put."

I got up and put on my hat and got to the door just as it

opened. Chas started to come in, head down, and I took him by the front of his coat and swung him off balance and laid one on his chin. He went to the floor and Bat Ears said:

"You couldn't do that if Chas wasn't high."

"Tell him that when he comes out of it," I said. "Don't tell me," and walked out.

I wanted no part of Chas, right at that time, and that seemed a good way of getting him out of the way.

CHUCK BARNETT WASN'T in his office, although it was ten the next morning before I called. His dopy looking office girl said he hadn't been in and that she didn't expect him until afternoon. She was a screwy looking tramp who labored under the delusion she was a honey and she smirked at me and said:

"Oh, Mr. Connell! Won't I do?"

"Not for what I want Chuck for."

She shook herself coyly and said, "Tee-hee."

I said, "All right, tee-hee. But you tell Chuck I was in and tell him to wear knucks to make it even the next time I see him. Tell him he's going to have a lot of gold teeth in the front of his face. He'll know what you mean."

She tittered and said, "You're such a joker."

"You mean joke," I said. "Tell Chuck that."

I looked back as I went through the door and she was looking as though somebody had taken her candy away from her. I thought that if she was silly enough to imagine I'd go for a line like hers she was as punch-drunk as Chuck Barnett would be when I was through with him. But I thought of something else and asked:

"Anything new about Ransom's murder?"

"I think that's what Mr. Barnett is checking now. The police were here; I think they're going to arrest those people. Those Willards. It seems funny to me; him getting killed in their house."

"That's why the cops didn't arrest them before. Ransom had no business being there and the cops can't figure any reason for him being killed. I don't doubt the Willards are tagged, wherever they go."

She shook her head, said, "I always just hated Mr. Ransom. He wasn't a gentleman like you, Mr. Connell. He always made passes at me."

I thought about the old saying regarding "the woman scorned" and left—before I laughed.

Then I telephoned Jake Abrams and found he was all right, except for a headache, and told him what I'd done and found out from Chas and his pal. I was fifteen minutes late for my appointment when I finally got to Willard's office.

It was very nice. There was a reception room with desks for two girls and both of the desks had brass name plates on them. One said Miss Markey and the other said Miss Conover and both the gals were there. Willard hadn't arrived yet, so I spent half an hour looking at the girls.

They were both pretty. The Markey girl was blond and the Conover girl was dark. I gave Willard credit for being a good picker, even though I was getting plenty red-headed about being kept waiting by him. I finally decided I could like the Markey girl the most, the Conover menace being too snaky and wise looking to be my type, and about the time I figured this out, Willard came in. At ten-forty-five.

He hung his hat and coat in a wardrobe and then pretended to see me. He shook hands and said:

"Oh hello, Connell. Come in my office."

He led the way into what looked more like a living-room than an office. Lounge, overstuffed chairs, and the rest of that sort of thing. We sat down and he broke out a bottle from a built-in refrigerator and I told him I didn't drink that early. He looked snooty and said:

"Some people don't," and took a drink that was plenty big. Then he asked:

"What did you want to see me about?"

I didn't like him and I didn't like his attitude any better. I said, "Nothing in particular. I just wanted to talk to you about those robberies and murders at your place and I didn't feel like going to jail to do it. I hate the visiting hours they make you keep."

"What d'ya mean?" he asked.

"The cops aren't happy about that murder. Just because you say you didn't know Ransom, doesn't mean it's true. They haven't picked you up yet because they want a case against you that won't flop. You're lying about not knowing Ransom and I know it. They will, shortly. They work slow but they work."

"As I told them, I didn't know this Ransom."

I watched him, even more closely. "And you don't know Chuck Barnett, either?"

He said, "Why, no," and his eyes didn't flicker in the slightest.

I said, "Well, if it's true, the cops'll probably think Ransom got a line on those rings of your wife's and was after them. Myself, I think he was blackmailing the both of you, on the insurance angle. It's your dice, mister."

I left then and got out in the outside office just as the buzzer on the Conover girl's desk rang. She got up and went in Willard's office and I looked at the name plate again.

Then I got the idea. I went outside and picked a nice spot to wait where they couldn't spot me. I didn't have to wait very long.

Probably half an hour. Then Willard and the Conover girl came out and got in a roadster and I picked a cab and said:

"Follow that roadster. The one with the guy and gal." I flashed my badge and the hacker grinned and said:

"Somebody cheating, huh?"

"And how!" I said.

They headed straight for a big apartment house on the Marino and we weren't half a block behind them when they stopped and hurried in the place. I paid off the hack and headed after them and a big doorman said:

"Whom do you wish to see?"

I said: "Police! What apartment has the Conover girl?"

He told me: "Four twenty-six," before he got himself together enough to find out whether I was police or not and by the time he'd figured it out I was inside and half-way to the fourth floor.

The apartment door was one of the fancy affairs that look as though they're made to keep anybody from finding out what the apartment number is, but I finally decided on 426 and rang the button.

The door opened and Willard said, "Why—ugh—" He started to close the door but by that time I had a gun in his stomach and he changed his mind. I said:

"It's your mistake for opening up. If you'd kept it closed I'd have had to get the law and a warrant."

He said, "I don't understand."

By this time I had him backed into the main room. The Conover babe was standing up and holding one hand over her mouth and the other over her breast. I said to her:

"Go ahead, kid. Scream, if you think it'll make you feel better."

She took both hands down and said, "I'm going to call the police."

"Go ahead and save me the bother," I said.

She sat down then. I put Willard by her and said, "You two aren't as smart as you should be. I don't much mind Barney Ransom getting knocked off, but that insurance business was rank."

Willard straightened in his chair and looked haughty and said, "You'll have to explain this."

"I intended to explain it. You couldn't figure out anything to wrap up that stuff with so you took a pill-box off the girl here. Then you dropped it in your own mail-box. The pill-box had the girl's name on it, you dope. That settles the whole mess."

He started to get up and I said, "Sit back there."

He did. Then he said, "Why, this is simply ridiculous."

"They use a rope in this State, for murderers," I said. "Laugh that one off, too."

Then somebody poked something in the back of my neck and said:

"Laugh this off yourself."

I DROPPED MY gun without being told and the thing went away from the back of my neck. I heard footsteps slither on the rug and turned my head and saw Chas backing away from me and toward the side of the room. He had a .45 automatic pointed my way and didn't look away from me when he said to Willard:

"You damn fool! If he had any brains at all, he'd have smarted that somebody was behind him when you stood up. That could have blown the thing right then."

The minute I'd seen it was Chas I'd started to think what a fool I'd been not to turn Chas and his friend over to Sergeant Keene. I should have known that anyone as dopy as this Chas wouldn't have stayed put in the place I'd told him to stay. I said:

"Where's your pal Thomas?"

He said, "In the can. He was wanted on an armed robbery charge and they got him. I was out when they got him. I saw they had a stake on the place when I went back, so I didn't go in."

He had his soft drawling voice going evenly and nice and his eyes didn't look as hazy as they had the last time I'd seen them. He was in better shape.

Willard said, "Connell probably put the cops on you and Thomas."

I said to Chas, "That isn't so. You better ditch that gun, fella. There isn't anything against you now, but if you play around with that there's liable to be plenty."

He talked right past me, but he didn't look away from me, while he did. He said to Willard, "All right, Mister. This bird's got you cold. What's it worth for me to do the business?"

The Conover girl said, "You—you mean—kill him?"

Chas laughed and I changed my mind about him. He was as high as he was the time before. Or maybe higher. Willard said to the girl, "But, honey, what else can we do?"

She said, "I suppose you're right," showing the true womanly spirit, and Willard said to Chas: "The most I can get right now is about three hundred dollars."

Chas shook his head, never taking his eyes from me.

"I can't possibly raise a cent more than three fifty. I can give you more later," Willard said.

"Get the three fifty. I'll wait here with him."

I said, "You cheap heel! I ought to be worth more than that."

Chas said, "We'll fix Connell now and then get the dough."

Chas was keeping his voice level and even but that was the only thing normal about him. He'd started to shake a little and his face had whitened and he looked like a crazy man. In a shape like that he'd have killed a man for three dollars and a half, much less three hundred and fifty.

Willard stood, looking sick about the entire business, and I stalled them both with:

"How does Chuck Barnett come in on the deal?"

"You damn fool!" Chas said, and actually laughed. "He was keeping cases on this guy's old lady."

"What d'ya mean?"

"He had to know what she was going to do, didn't he? So Barnett tagged her for Willard. That's what I mean."

"I'll get the dough now," Willard said and walked forward. Chas was holding the gun so that it pointed at my shoulder. I took a chance, and just as Willard got even with me I dropped down and got hold of his knees and rolled. I tried to keep him in front of me, while I dragged him back to where I could get at my gun, which was on the floor where I'd dropped it.

Chas shot once while I was in the air—and missed. Then, while Willard and I were putting on our rolling act on the floor, he tried again. He missed me but not Willard. I felt Willard jerk in my arms and then quit trying to get away from me. At the same time I managed to reach out and get my gun. The girl tried to kick it out of my hand and Chas shot again.

He was good—but in the wrong way. The girl came down on this one. Chas was proving what's almost always true—that a man that's doped up will shoot before he's set for it. I was figuring a lot on that when I started the rumpus.

I shot three times then and I didn't miss him with any of them. He started to fall with the first one and by the time the third slug hit him he was on the floor. I got away from Willard, got Chas' gun, and saw he was dead. There was no mistake. One of the slugs had hit him in the chin and left no doubt.

I looked at the girl then. She was sitting on the floor and looking at the side of her thigh and I saw the slug had just creased her hard enough to throw her off her feet. I said:

"Pretty leg!"

She said: "You ——!" and kept staring at her leg. I looked at Willard and saw he'd taken his ticket high in the shoulder and was out from the shock. A .45, that close, will do it every time it hits a bone. For that matter, lots of times when it doesn't. There's force behind a chunk of lead that big.

I went to the phone and called Sergeant Keene and told him to come up with the ambulance and the dead wagon. He said:

"Who is it this time?"

I said, "Come on up and find out. Bring Kitty with you."

"Why him?"

"I want to hear him meauw," I said.

I went to the hall door and told the manager, who was raising hell there, to keep his shirt on and that everything was under control. That the law had been called and that everything was kosher.

KEENE DIDN'T HAVE a great deal to say to me until Willard and the girl had been started to the hospital with a police guard on them. The minute they were gone, before Chas had been carted away or anything, he waved toward another room and said:

"In here, Connell."

I followed him in and said, "Sure, the star chamber session, huh! Let me call Jake Abrams first, though."

"To hell with Abrams," he said. "What's he got to do with this?"

"It was his company that was insuring the stuff that Willard stole from his wife. Abrams will be interested."

Keene snorted and said, "Who shot who?"

"Chas, the dead man out there, shot Willard and the gal. I shot Chas. You check the slugs and they'll prove it."

He grunted and said, "What was Chas doing here? That's a hell of a name. Chas!"

"It stands for Charles. You've got a guy named Thomas, down in the can. Well, Willard got Chas and Thomas to get me out of the way for a while. Mrs. Willard hired me, over Willard's protests, and he didn't want me hanging around. Then, as I see it, Chas figured he had Willard over a barrel and came up here to roll him a bit. I walked in and upset things and Chas propositioned Willard for a job getting rid of me."

"How much did he want to do the job?"

"Three fifty."

Keene laughed and said, "Too much."

The moment I'd told him three fifty I knew I'd made a mistake. He'll rib me the rest of my life over that. I went on with: "Willard swiped his wife's rings and let her collect from the insurance company. He needed the dough, she as much as told me that. Then, when she got it, he gave her some cock and bull story and had her bring the money home and then he swiped that as well. She didn't come out and say that and that's why I know she thought he did it. She wanted to protect him, which is natural. And easy to figure out. And then, he returned the stuff and turned her in to the insurance company for stealing her own jewelry. He called them up and said it was a phony. He's that sort of a heel."

Keene looked as though I was telling fairy stories and asked, "Why would he do a screwy stunt like that to his own wife?"

"He's stuck for this Conover tart and by turning his old lady in he would get her out of the way and have the insurance money besides. The damned fool even took the stuff back in a box with the Conover woman's name on it."

Keene looked thoughtful. Then asked, "What about Ransom? I want the guy that killed him."

"Willard had Ransom and Barnett following his wife to see what she was going to do. That'll show in their office records. Ransom must have gone out to Willard's house to make a report, and my guess is he tried a little blackmail on the side. On his own hook. About the insurance company angle. Then Willard laid him low and called his sweetie, back at the office, to alibi him. That's the only answer. When you get Willard so he can answer questions, find that out. It had to be him."

Keene shook his head, as though that was the way it looked to him, and said, "He'll talk. And the Conover gal will talk. She's in it, too."

I said, "Willard will probably beat the rap on it. If he can show Ransom was blackmailing him, the jury will be on his side."

"He'll stand trial, anyway," Keene said. "That's all I'm supposed to do; put 'em up there in court with a case against 'em."

I said, "Oke by me. You coming with me while I talk to Mrs. Willard?"

"Why should I?"

I said, "I've done all your work for you on this. You ought to go along and give me a hand now. She isn't going to feel good at all when I tell her about her old man."

He sighed and stood up and said, "Well, I guess one good turn—and the rest of it."

I'd done a good turn for Keene when I wrecked the Chas man for him. I'd done a good turn for Abrams and his company when I hooked Willard and the Conover girl. For that matter, they'd even found most of the insurance money in la Conover's apartment and had claimed it.

And then Ransom got killed and that was a good turn for the city. The only one that didn't win was me—I barely made expenses. I even ended up with a broken hand... I met Chuck Barnett one night and remembered I didn't like him very much.

That was another good turn, if it comes to that. For the doctor that patched up Chuck's broken-jaw.

Relative Trouble

Death plays a fast tune for Shean Connell

HE WAS HALF in and half out of my piano when I saw him, and I left him there until the cops came. Moving him wouldn't have helped him one bit and the cops like to have their corpses left in a natural state. Or an unnatural state, if that's what it is.

I'd been playing the little grand piano that morning, and I'd left the cover up and the music stand pushed back against it. That left an open space over the hammers and action and this dead man had the upper part of his body draped over this space. One foot was on the floor and his other knee was on the piano bench. He'd butted the rack with his head and loose music sheets had fallen over him and sopped up part of the blood. But not all of it; even the rug hadn't been able to do that. He'd been stabbed at least a dozen times in the face, the neck, and in the back. I didn't look too closely, not wanting to move him, but from what I could see none of the wounds were deep.

I called the station and got Sergeant Keene who's on Homicide. I said, "This is Shean Connell. I just came home and found a stiff in my place. Thought I'd better tell you about it."

I could hear him say something to somebody in his office and then he said to me, in a funny sort of voice: "Say, is this a rib?"

I said, "Hell, no! I bought a new piano this month and I think the thing's wrecked. The stiff bled into it. It cost me damn near a thousand bucks and if you think I rib about that kind of dough, you're nuts."

"Kitt and Mahlon are already on their way up there," he said.

"They left ten minutes ago—when I got the call."

"What call?"

He spaced his words out, as though he didn't want to make any mistake. "Ten minutes ago. To be exact, at four thirty-seven P.M., some woman called in and I took it. She reported you were dead. She refused to give her name. I had her call checked and it was from a pay phone in a drugstore that has four booths and all doing business. I figured it was a gag but I sent Kitt and Mahlon to check. They should be there now."

I live in an apartment hotel that has a bar. I reminded Keene of this and said, "That's where they probably are. Kitt don't like any part of me and he's probably planted on a bar stool drinking to the chances of finding me stiff."

"I'm coming out. Who's the dead man, Shean?"

I said, "He's about thirty-five and he weighs close to two hundred pounds. He's dark. He looks pretty prosperous. Outside of that, I don't know a thing about him."

Somebody started pounding on the door and I told Keene this and he said again that he was coming out. I suggested he do it, instead of talk about it, and hung up. And then went to the door and let in Kitt and Mahlon.

Kitt is overgrown. Physically, not mentally. He weighs two

hundred and forty pounds and the only fat is in his head. Even his brother cops know him for a heel and they're a clannish tribe, usually. Mahlon is little and short and kewpie looking. Quite a paunch. A swell guy who wouldn't have a thing to do with Kitt if he didn't have to on account of the job. They're paired, so Mahlon hasn't an out. I've always hated Kitt's very insides and Kitt knows it.

The big clown loomed there in the door and gawked at me and said, "Hey! We thought you was dead."

I said I was sorry to disappoint him but that he could see for himself the rumor was exaggerated.

He said, "Cracking all the time, huh! I'll crack you some-time," and then stalked over and looked at the corpse.

Mahlon said, "Never mind him, Shean! He's been on his ear all day."

"Somebody ought to give the big heel catnip."

Kitt heard this one and turned around. Naturally he's called Kitty for a nickname, but damn few people do it to his face because he's so big. He growled something to Mahlon, went to the phone and called the station. He found that Sergeant Keene was already on his way, along with the photographer, the Medical Examiner, and the rest of the help, and then swung around to me and said, "What did you do it with, Connell?"

"My bread knife. It's in the kitchenette," I said.

He opened one door and found the bathroom, then another and found the clothes closet. The only other door in the place was the one they'd entered from the hall. He stared around the place, as though I had a kitchenette hid under the couch, then snapped:

"You ain't got any kitchenette. Bread knife, hell!"

"I must have done it with a paring knife then. That's in the kitchenette, too. All you've got to do is find a kitchenette."

Mahlon said, "Leave him alone, Kitt. Keene's on the way. You and Connell don't get along, anyway."

Then Keene came, with the technical crew, which saved some harsh words, probably. The M.E. looked the body over, looking more puzzled all the time, then said:

"Apparently this man bled to death. He's been stabbed four-teen separate times, and three of the wounds would have been fatal. But certainly not instantly so. I don't understand this."

Keene asked why not. The M.E. lifted one of the dead

man's hands, pointed out: "There's no marks here and there would have been if he'd tried to defend himself. That's almost a certainty. A big husky man wouldn't let himself be cut to pieces without defending himself and leaving some evidence of it on his hands. It's all wrong. And the stab wounds are shallow; that's odd. It's a puzzle."

I'd been looking over the body, while he was doing the talking to Keene. I said, "I suppose it'll take an autopsy to show it plainly, but if the back of this guy's head isn't caved in a bit, I'm wrong."

The doc got red in the face and looked at the man's head. And then admitted that the man had undoubtedly been unconscious while the cutting went on. Keene listened to this, then said to me: "I can't see what difference it makes. He's dead, ain't he?"

"I can't see any difference either," I said. "I never saw the man in my life before. I don't know his name or what he was doing here. I can't understand how he got in my room, even. The hotel wouldn't let a stranger in, unless I okayed it. All I get out of this is my new piano ruined."

Kitt was listening to this wail. He made himself look even uglier than usual, by scowling, and said, "That ain't all you get out of it by a damn sight. Doc says this bird's been dead about two hours and you get a chance to prove an alibi for yourself around that time. You get a chance to tell about this at the inquest. You're going to get trouble out of this, mister, and don't forget it. If I can tie you in with this, it'll be big trouble."

I said, "Meauw, meauw, meauw."

Keene said, "I'm taking care of it, Kitt."

Then we all rode to the station. Even the corpse went down, but he rode by himself in the dead wagon.

SERGEANT KEENE PUT a picture of the man in the papers for a start and the doctor did a post-mortem in order to have no doubt about what the man had died from. Nobody answered the paper stuff and we went into the inquest without knowing who he was or what he was doing in my apartment.

The first on the stand was the doctor. Then myself. Then Kitt, Mahlon, and Keene. Keene told about trying to find who the man was and the rest of that. The jurors asked him a few questions. Inquests are informal as a rule, and I could see where the questions were leading. Keene got the idea right along with me. He came out with:

"I'll now state I checked Mr. Connell's time for that afternoon and he was miles from his apartment at the time the murder was committed. In my opinion, Mr. Connell is as much mystified about the affair as we are. Mr. Connell has promised us his help, in case he happens on any information about this matter."

That ended the hearing. The jurors decided on the usual "death by unknown person or persons" and it was over. But just as Keene and I were climbing into the squad car we'd ridden down in, one of the jurors came up. He was a little sharp-faced egg and he ran a little hot dog stand right on the edge of town. He said, "Say, Sergeant, there was something I meant to ask and didn't think of it at the time. D'ya remember what that dead man looked like?"

Keene said he remembered perfectly.

The little man screwed up his face, said: "All I saw was his picture in the paper. But if that guy didn't look like Connell, here, I'm all wet. Is it an idea or not?"

Keene said, "Well, by ——! That's what I was trying to think

of all the time. Same weight, same coloring, and all. If you didn't know Connell, this guy could have passed on Connell's description."

He asked me what I thought and I said it hadn't occurred to me. That the only time I looked in the glass was when I shaved. The little juror grinned at us and said, "Well, think it over, boys."

We did, and it didn't mean a thing to either of us. I wasn't working on anything that could lead into murder, as far as I knew, anyway. And there was still the question about how the guy got in my place; nobody in the hotel seemed to know a thing about that.

And there was something else that puzzled me. The Medical Examiner had said the smash the man had taken across the head was a slanting blow, running down the head from left to right. From about the center of his head and slanting down toward his right ear. This had me a bit puzzled, even though Keene apparently hadn't noticed it.

Keene drove me to my apartment and I got out. Linda Wilson was waiting for me when I got up to my rooms. She'd been worried about the inquest, even though I hadn't been. I'd been running around with her quite some time—in fact long enough so that she had a key to my place and a standing invitation to use it often.

She was sitting on the piano bench, not knowing that was where I'd found the dead man, and she was fooling around the piano keys without looking at them.

"Hello, hon! What's the matter?" I asked.

She kept on noodling with the piano and said, "Do I look that bad? Like something was the matter?"

She didn't look as good as she usually did but I wasn't fool enough to say so. I told her she looked like a million dollars as always and that the inquest went along fine and that there was no trouble at all about the man being found dead in my place. That there'd never been a suspicion of trouble for me on that.

She listened to all this, still fooling around on the piano. She happened to hit a note that sounded muffled and odd, and I said, just to change the subject:

"Keep your hand there, hon! There's something wrong with that key."

I looked, saw it was the F natural below middle C and then looked in the piano. There was a paper book of matches jammed into the three wires of the note and I dug them out and saw the packet was lettered Wrigley's Spearmint Gum, which didn't mean a thing. The piano had been cleaned after the man had been killed on it, but the cleaning had been done with the idea of getting the blood away. Linda watched me get this match cover out, then said:

"You're going to hate me, Shean, for what I'm going to tell you. I let that man in your apartment. I know who he is and what he wanted. I was afraid to tell you; afraid I'd be dragged into it."

"Who was he?" I asked. "Don't you know a thing like that will always come out?"

She shrugged her shoulders and got away from the piano. She said, "All right, it was this way. It just happens you killed my stepfather when he was about to kill an innocent person. You know that. You know there's been a lot of talk about you and me, because of that. You did the right thing, but it hasn't made things easy for Mother or myself. Now suppose I got mixed up in this? It would be just that much more fuel added to the fire. I naturally would have told what I'd done if it had been necessary; if you had trouble about this. That's why I've been so worried. Now I can tell you and that's all there is to it."

Linda isn't the nervous type and I didn't get the idea. I said, "Why, what the hell, hon! Why didn't you tell me about the guy? What's the difference? I didn't have anything to do with the guy; I couldn't get in trouble over him. Who was he?"

She said, "My uncle, or my dead stepfather's brother, rather. He came from Omaha and found out how Dad had been killed. He somehow found that I had a key to your place. Maybe from Mother; she was terribly afraid of him just the same as she was afraid of my stepfather. He made me let him in. I waited outside, to tell you about him, but you drove up in a cab and ducked in before I could stop you. That's all. You found him dead, and I was afraid that if I told who he was, it would just make it worse for all of us."

"But, honey, he had nothing against me."

"He thought he had, Shean. He meant to do you harm. He didn't say that but I know it."

She started to cry, saying I'd never like her again and a bunch of foolishness like that. I soothed her down, mainly by telling her she'd probably kept me out of a bunch of trouble, and she finally got calm enough to go home.

It left me in a hell of a spot. The man, she'd told me his name was Augustus Morrison Wilson, had been slugged and then knifed fourteen times. Linda was husky enough to slug him and knock him out. And the knife stabs, every one shallow and only three in a definitely fatal place, looked more like woman's work than man's.

She'd told the truth about me coming home in a cab and ducking fast in the place. I remembered that. But I'd run around with the girl for almost a year and I knew the temper she had. I knew how crazy she was about her mother and she'd admitted this dead man had frightened her mother badly. She could have let him in my place and bopped him with something and stabbed him; then waited downstairs for me.

For that matter, if she'd thought he was bad medicine for me she might have done him in on that account. I didn't put it past her for a minute. The girl was emotional and nobody knew it better than I. I decided I'd better not say anything to Keene about it, at least until I'd had time to figure things out a bit. Linda was entitled to protection. She had quite a lot of money, and money is back of a lot of trouble. She didn't handle it herself; George Thompson, a lawyer, was in charge of it, but he gave her what she wanted when she wanted it. The only thing was, she gave it away as fast as she got it, keeping a bunch of relatives as well as running a sort of private relief agency. People like that are entitled to all they can get.

I WASN'T THE only one with ideas but I didn't find that out until about twelve that night. The phone rang and somebody said, "Connell? Is this Shean Connell?"

I said it was but I'd just came out of a sound sleep and I probably mumbled. Because the voice snapped, "Speak up, man. Are you Connell?"

"Yes. Who's talking?"

"A friend of yours."

"Now listen," I said, "If you think I like to wake up in the middle of the night to play guessing games you can try another think. Who in the hell is it?"

"A friend, I said. A good friend. Both of you and your girl."

"That's fine. But who are you?" I was wide awake after that last crack, but I kept trying to sound as sleepy as before.

"Never you mind who. I've been a good enough friend not to go to the cops with what I know about Gus Wilson and that girl of yours. If that means anything."

I said, "Who's Gus Wilson?" and buzzed the desk on the house phone that stood on the same stand by my bed. All I could get on the house phone was the desk, bar, dining-room, and so on, and I wanted any one of them.

The outside phone said, "You know who Gus Wilson is," just as the house phone said, "Desk clerk. Mr. Emmond speaking."

I said to the first: "Don't gag with me. I don't know what you're talking about," then held my hand over that mouth-piece and said into the other: "Mr. Emmond! Have the call that's coming in through the board checked. Have the operator tell the supervisor it's police business. Hurry on it, man. It's important."

The first phone said, "Gus Wilson is the guy who was found dead in your apartment. The guy your girl killed. Now do you know what I'm talking about?"

"You must be nuts, whoever you are," I said.

"So I'm nuts, eh? O.K., smart guy. She went into your place with this bird two hours before you got home. She was in with him there about fifteen minutes, not less. She came out, looking goofy as hell. If it comes to a question, the hotel help will remember her, I don't doubt. They're used to seeing her and don't pay any attention to her ordinarily but they'll remember if they're asked about it. She went downstairs and waited for you and missed you. I know all this and I can let the cops in on it if it isn't supposed to be a secret."

I tried to keep the man on the wire to give the tracer business a chance. I said, "Well, I didn't know about that. If it's so, she probably has an explanation."

"Sure she'll have. But it won't be one the cops'll believe."

I didn't say anything for a moment and he said, "Say! You there? You listening?"

I said I was still listening.

"You aren't trying any smart stuff like trying to trace this call?"

"Don't be a dope! How could I as long as you're on the wire?"

This seemed to satisfy him. He went on with: "I'm not the guy to call copper on a right guy. Get the idea?"

I got the idea and asked, "How much?"

The voice got jeering. "How much you got?"

"I could maybe raise twelve or fifteen hundred."

"You could probably raise about three times that, guy. I been checking on you. And the girl could get as much more and I know that, too. She's got money and so has her mother."

"How much d'ya want?"

"I'll call you back and tell you."

"When? When will you call?"

Whoever it was laughed. "When you don't expect it. And I'll call from a pay phone so don't bother to check it."

The phone clicked in my ear then. I got the house phone and the desk and said: "Did you get that call?"

The voice said, very patiently: "Why yes, Mr. Connell. That was from the Central Police Station. The operator was unable to discover who it was, however."

I said, "That's all right. I can tell you. It was from a big heel named Kitt."

I got Linda's house on the phone then, and a sleepy maid said she'd call her. She didn't sound nearly as sleepy five minutes later, when she said, "I'm sorry, Mr. Connell, but Miss Linda isn't home. I understand she was to meet you."

"What's that?"

"Why, yes. She came home, after seeing you, but when you called she left again. I'm Felice, the maid, and I heard her mention it to her mother."

I said, "Thank you, Felice," and hung up. The voice that had asked for blackmail had sounded a bit odd and not like Kitt's, but he could have changed it by speaking through a handkerchief or by holding a coin in his mouth. I'd walked into something, that was a cinch. And Linda was squarely into it as well.

I figured Kitt had been doing some guessing and some gumshoe work and some adding two and two and getting five. It had to be Kitt. Mahlon was just a side man, with no particular reason to go on with the thing on his own hook, and Kitt had the personal feeling against me to spur him on. Keene was out of it; he was a friend and he'd have put his cards on the table and had a showdown if he'd suspected Linda.

FORTY MINUTES LATER I was at the Central Station, but neither Kitt nor Mahlon were there. They'd been there, but left no word where they were going, as both were off duty and had been off duty all day.

I was talking to Joe Beecher, the sergeant on the desk, and he told me this and then said, "They brought in that guy and then took him out with them. He was a dopy looking bird, too."

"What guy? What are you talking about?" I asked, trying to figure where Linda would be if Kitt and Mahlon didn't have her. I knew most of her friends but it's not a good idea calling people at a quarter to one in the morning and asking about your girl. It makes talk and there was enough talk already.

Joe Beecher said, "I don't know his name. They never booked him so we haven't got him on the records. He was a sort of wacky looking bird. Looked like a country boy and talked like one. Dopy, sort of. Like he was off a farm, if you know what I mean."

I tumbled then. Joe was trying to tell me something. So I said I knew and asked what Kitt and Mahlon had been working on lately. Beecher gave me a funny look and said:

"I wouldn't know, Shean! But you've got to admit that business up in your apartment didn't look good at all."

I said: "Thanks!" and he looked blank and said, "For what? I didn't tell you anything."

"Of course not, Joe. Sometime I'll buy a cigar or a drink."

"And she isn't here, either, Shean. If you know what I mean. They could hold her here for a while without booking her, but she isn't here."

"I get it," I said. "I'll get a lawyer and I'll have her out in two hours if I wake up every judge in town."

Beecher grinned and said, "Try Raoul LeFevre first. He prides himself on being the real type of French gentleman and he'll go to bat for injured womanhood every time. He'll honor a writ for you, or I miss my guess."

I said, "Thanks!" and left. In a hurry.

I had to get a lawyer but the more I thought of it the less I thought I'd need a writ. If Kitt and Mahlon were sure of what they were doing, they'd have charged Linda right off the bat, instead of working the gag they had. I figured Kitt was doing a lot of guessing and wasn't sure he could prove any of the answers. So I dug up Aaron Weidman, who costs money but is good, and told him what I wanted and we started out.

We found Linda in the third precinct we tried. Mahlon was sitting in the main room, talking to part of the riot squad who were waiting for some excitement to come in, and he looked up and saw me and stammered.

"Why—why, hello, Connell."

Mahlon's got red rosy cheeks but they didn't have much color. They'd faded a bit. His voice is a nice tenor, ordinarily, but now it sounded a bit squeaky.

I said: "All right! Where is she? And where's Kitt?"

He started to say something, then looked at me and then at Weidman, who has a reputation of keeping on after starting something. I was moving in close, right then, figuring to smack him if he started a stall. There were five cops in the room, but I knew I'd get in at least one good lick and, the way I felt, one good lick would be worth the beating I'd take right after I landed it. I'd always liked Mahlon and I knew he was in this because Kitt was insisting on it, but I wasn't thinking of that right then.

Mahlon said, "She's in the back, Shean! Now don't fly off the handle. The matron's with her. She's been treated fine. She hasn't been charged and there's been nothing she can complain about. She'll tell you that herself."

"Let her tell me then."

Mahlon started toward the door, leading to the back, and I said to Weidman: "Come on, counselor."

Mahlon said, "There's no need of trouble, Shean. You don't need a lawyer."

I said, "Come on," to Weidman, again and the two of us followed Mahlon to the back.

Linda was sitting on a chair but there were no trick lights on her. The matron was sitting back of her, working on what looked like the "little garments" the young bride coyly shows the young husband in the story books. Kitt was sitting on a table, swinging one leg back and forth, and staring at Linda as though he wasn't able to make up his mind what to do with her. All three of them turned when we came in the room and Linda said:

"I knew you'd be here, Shean. I've been telling this big hippo that."

"Has he bothered you?"

"Sure. Of course he has."

I made a dive toward Kitt but Weidman had apparently been expecting just that. He's short and blocky and built like a Shetland pony, and he caught me from behind, wrapping his arms around me. Kitt swung off the table, saying, "Let him loose! I'm ready for him."

Weidman was saying in my ear: "Now Connell. Listen! Wait! Don't make this bad! Now wait!"

Mahlon got in between Kitt and me, and the matron waddled over to the door that led to the outer room, and called: "A couple of you boys come in here."

Linda said, "That's not the way I meant it, Shean. He and this man," she pointed at Mahlon, "just brought me here and threatened to arrest me for killing Gus Wilson. They know he was my stepfather's brother and they seem to think I killed him."

Two men from the riot squad were in the room by then and I'd quieted down. Kitt was big enough to make me enough trouble, without fighting the rest of the police force in addition.

Weidman said to Kitt, "Is this right, officer?"

Kitt said he guessed it was, but he didn't sound very sure of himself. Weidman got the angle and pounced on him with: "I demand you either release this young lady at once or charge her with murder. This is outrageous!"

Kitt muttered something about being able, legally, to hold her so many hours without booking her and Weidman grinned, very nastily, at him and said, "I'm sure Judge LeFevre will appreciate that statement, sir. I only hope you'll repeat it when you're up before the police board charged with exceeding your duty and with conduct unbecoming an officer."

Kitt wasn't afraid of the police board one bit but he didn't have a cinch case and he was afraid to go to bat without one. He said grudgingly, "It's all right, Miss Wilson. You can go home now. But I'd advise you not to leave town or anything like that." Then he gave me a dirty look and finished with: "And I'd advise you not to have anything to do with Connell, either. You'd never have been suspected in this matter if it hadn't been for him. He just the same as admitted you know more than you've told us."

I hit him then but he'd been waiting for it and rolled with the smack. He slammed back at me and I ducked it. I hit him again, pretty low in the stomach. He caught me high on the cheek with a left and it shook me up a bit. Everybody in the room, including Linda, got between us. Then we all left, with Weidman saying loudly and viciously:

"A gross abuse of police power."

We had coffee before we took Linda home and I told Weidman the story. Right from the start. I left out my own idea about Linda possibly killing her uncle, of course, but he got the angle and said:

"Did you kill the man, Miss Wilson? A self-defense plea would clear you, in all probability, if you could show the man had threatened you. I imagine, from what you've said, this wouldn't be hard to do. A jury would recognize the fact of your being in fear of your life."

Linda jerked her head up and stared at him. "I certainly did not kill him. It happened just as I told Shean. Exactly that way."

She turned her head and saw my face. "That's what you thought, too, Shean Connell! I can see that now."

Of course I said I didn't and hadn't thought any such thing. Weidman listened with a grin to this. Then he said to me:

"Suppose we take the young lady home. The best thing you can do, Connell, is find the real killer. I'm sure the police won't be satisfied until the killer is found."

"I balled it up when I talked to Kitt over the phone," I said.

"You surely did," Weidman agreed. "Kitt did a smart trick there; pretending to do a little blackmail and finding out you seemed willing to go for the idea. That was smart."

I hadn't told Linda all about this part of it. I did then. She said: "Did you mean to pay them, Shean?"

"I guess so."

Weidman said, "And on account of that very willingness of yours to pay, Kitt is fairly certain Miss Wilson did the killing. It's an unfortunate situation."

I said, "That's a miracle of understatement. Come on, Linda, we'll take you home."

BREAKING EVEN WITH Kitt was the first thing to do; to find out where he got his information and to see how much guessing he was doing. I moved around my hotel and found he'd talked to a couple of bellboys and clerks, but none of them had told him a thing that meant anything. They'd said that Miss Linda Wilson occasionally visited me, which didn't mean a thing. For that matter, they didn't seem to realize she had her own key to my place, and this wasn't at all odd. I'd had a duplicate made for her from my own just so there'd be no talk in the hotel.

There'd been enough talk already, the way I figured it, because of her running around with me after I'd been forced to shoot her stepfather. Nobody seemed to realize Linda and her mother had both hated and feared the man and that the action had been forced on me.

I sent a wire back to an agency I knew of in Omaha and hoped for results from the check-up on Gus Wilson I'd asked for. But they were handicapped; they had no more idea of what they were to look for than I had. All they could possibly send me was his record, if any, and past history. Maybe a list of associates.

I was sitting at the piano, just fooling around with a bunch of old music and thinking this over. Then I happened to think of the matches I'd found in the wires and that I'd noticed something funny about them. I dug them out of the drawer I'd tossed them in and looked them over and discovered what was funny about them.

Right-handed people hold a paper packet of matches in their left hand and pull them off from the right of the packet. This packet was half empty and the empty side was on the left. It didn't mean anything much right then, but it didn't make me feel any better because I remembered Linda was lefthanded.

It was about three in the afternoon then and the desk called and said Sergeant Keene was downstairs. By the time Keene got up I had a couple of drinks set out and met him at the door with a big hello on top of them. I didn't know whether he was coming in war or peace and I wanted him to know I wanted peace.

Apparently he did. He gave me a sort of sheepish grin and said, "Hell, Shean, I'm sorry about what that heel of a Kitt did. Believe me, if I'd known he was going to pull a screwy act like that, I'd have knocked his ears down."

"I tried," I said, "but I didn't get far. The guy's so damn big it's like hitting a horse."

He sat down with his drink and I got him another when the first was gone. Then he came out with what he was really there to find out. He said, very casually, "Who told you the boys had Linda and where she was held?"

"Nobody told me," I said, trying to look innocent. "I just figured it out. You know about Kitt calling me, don't you?"

"He told me something about it. That looks bad, Shean, I'll tell you."

"It doesn't mean a thing. I figured somebody was trying to pull a fast one and I was going to toll 'em along until I could get my hands on 'em. I hate a blackmailer more than I do a killer. I knew Linda was in the clear, but I thought I could stall and act scared and catch me somebody."

Keene looked as though he wanted to believe this but couldn't quite do it. I went on with: "And, of course, as soon as I recognized Kitt's voice, I knew what the score was. He'd got a screwy idea and was trying to play me against the gal. I hung up on him right then and started out looking the stations over for the girl."

"He didn't tell me you hung up on him or that you recognized his voice. I guess it doesn't make any difference anyway, Shean. I can't imagine that nice little girl of yours killing anybody. Though I'll admit Kitt and Mahlon have the notion she did it."

"What was the idea of asking who told me Kitt and Mahlon had Linda?"

Of course he figured there'd been a leak in the department and, to a cop, this is a terrible thing. He proved me right when he said: "Now listen, Shean! I'm not upholding Kitt and Mahlon for what they did. I took them both over the hurdles about it this morning, just as soon as I found out about it. But if any other cop stooled on them, whether they were right or wrong, I'll have his buttons inside of twenty-four hours. If we don't stick together in our own organization, we'd lose fifty per cent of our efficiency. It's my duty to check on that."

"I know it, Sarge," I said, thinking what a swell guy Joe Beecher was to give me the tip he had and take such chances. "But I figured it out with my own little mind. Have another drink."

He did, and then left. And left a thought. Thinking about Joe Beecher had reminded me about what Beecher had said about Kitt and Mahlon having a prisoner and not booking him. About him being a country-looking boy and dopy and all that. And thinking about this country stuff reminded me about Linda's dead stepfather once having a country place up at Pinehurst and that Pinehurst was country if ever there was such a thing.

I called Linda and got her just as she was getting out of the bathtub. She snapped, "I'm meeting you in two hours, you goop. Why don't you give me a chance to get prettied up for it? I've got a towel around me and that's all."

"That's all right," I said. "Television's in the future, hon. Have you had any company from Pinehurst lately? Has anybody called to pay their respects?"

She said she didn't know and sounded curious about why I'd asked. I said, "O.K. I'll ask your mother. Meet you in two hours."

She said, "I'll call her," which she didn't have to do. I could have got the number again and the maid would have put Linda's mother on the wire over an extension and Linda knew this full well. All that was the matter was she wanted to hear what I had to say to Mother.

I could hear the phone clank down on the stand, then hear Linda bawling, very faintly, "Mother! Mother! Shean wants to talk with you. It's important."

Then she came back and said, very sweetly: "Where you taking me to dinner, Shean?"

I said: "Harry's Chop House. It's cheap and they serve big orders. What more can you ask."

She called me what's almost a fighting word and then her mother said, "Hello, Shean. What is it?"

"Do you know whether anybody from Pinehurst is in town, Mrs. Wilson? Did anybody happen to call you?"

She said, doubtfully, "Now I don't think— Yes, somebody called but neither Linda nor I were at home. They didn't leave their name and the maid neglected to ask for it. Shean, Linda told me about last night. Is she in trouble over that?"

I lied, "Of course not," and said I'd call again.

Then I got the Ben Levy agency on the phone, got Ben himself, and said, "Ben, you got any good leg men wearing out their pants around the office?"

He said the way business was with his agency, that's all any of them ever did.

"Fine, Ben. Have about five of them cut the town in sections and check every hotel. Just look the register over and find if anybody is registered from Pinehurst. If they find anybody, have them get a fairly good description and you get in touch with me."

WHEN LINDA MET me we went to Harry's Chop House, and then saw a lousy picture in which the crooks talked as though they'd learned their dialogue in Harvard. We got back to my place about eleven. There were three telephone slips waiting for me—all with a message to call Mr. Ben Levy at his office.

I did and he said, "I get the dope you ask me for and you don't stay home to get it. We got a Pinehurst man for you. Name's Millard Brower. He's at the Traveler's Hotel."

I told Ben to send me the bill and pray he'd collect, and then asked Linda who Millard was.

She began to laugh. "Millard Brower is the boy who used to deliver the groceries to our lodge. When we lived there in Pinehurst, I mean. He's just a big kid that gets red in the face when anybody looks at him. I spoke to him once and he got his feet tangled up and fell down and broke two dozen eggs. He seems like a nice kid but he's so bashful it's painful to be around him."

I said: "O.K., hon, you can go home. I'm going to be busy."

"Doing what?"

"Calling on your friend Millard Brower. I want to see if he falls over his feet when I talk to him."

"I'll go with you."

When I thought this over it didn't seem a bad idea. I said, "The idea is, hon, that Kitt and Mahlon found out things about you and your family. I don't know just where, but they had some country-looking kid with them earlier in the day. They didn't book this kid, just talked to him."

We went to the Traveler's Hotel, a cheap joint well on the edge of town; the kind of place a country boy would pick if he was trying to save his money. Millard was in 217, according to the clerk, and I knocked on the door and nudged Linda when somebody said:

"Who is it?"

"It's me. Linda Wilson," she said.

He said: "Wait a minute," and opened the door five minutes later, still buttoning the collar of his shirt. He was a tall gangling kid and he was already blushing. Linda introduced me and he said:

"I—I—ugh, saw Mr. Connell when he was in Pinehurst."

I said, "That makes it easy then, bud. Just what did you tell the cops?"

"They told me I wasn't to tell anybody about that."

Linda smiled nicely at him and said: "But you'll tell me, won't you, Millard?"

Millard got fiery red and said he would. And did. He'd called the Wilson house, to pay his respects to Mrs. Wilson and Linda. He didn't have to say he had a wild case of love for

Linda; that stuck out all over him and I thought it was funny. He'd phoned but neither Linda nor her mother were home and the kid didn't have anything to do so he wandered over to their house. The worshiping the idol from afar idea. He saw Linda come out, with somebody he recognized as her stepfather's brother, and he followed them. I gathered the idea was he wanted to speak to Linda and was too bashful to do it in front of anyone else.

They went to my place and he tagged them. They went upstairs and he waited around and saw Linda come back downstairs alone. He saw her wait around the front of the place, but by that time the bashfulness had him in such shape he'd changed his mind about talking with her. Just a big dopy kid.

"How did you get in touch with Kitt, the policeman, and why did you do that?" I asked.

"I saw Mr. Wilson's picture in the paper. I told the police about that, the way the paper said to do. I talked with a man named Kitt and a man named Mahlon. They told me to say nothing about it to anybody else."

I said, without much hope: "And that's all you saw? Linda and this man Wilson going upstairs and then Linda coming down alone?"

"Well, I guess so. Of course there was the man that was in the fight. I saw him."

"What's this?"

"Well, while Miss Linda and Wilson were upstairs a car drove up and parked right by where I was standing. A man got out and walked to the back of the apartment house. A little man, looked like a Filipino. Two other men stayed in the car. Then Miss Linda came out and sort of waited around and then by and by this little man came back from where he'd gone. He'd been in a fight, because there was blood all over him. He was a little bit of a fellow. One of the other men had left the car while this little fellow had been gone. I noticed that, too."

The kid showed me how small the man had been by holding his hand about four feet from the floor.

I said, "Oke. This does it, but just what it does I don't know."

I told the kid to get his hat and coat on and that he was going to the police station. On the way down to the station I said:

"Did you tell Kitt and Mahlon about seeing this little man?"

"Why now, I don't think I did. They never asked me about him."

KEENE WAS IN the Homicide room and I took the kid in to him. I said, "Look, Sergeant, here's a guy that saw the killer five minutes after he did the killing. Have you got a little short guy in the files, looking like a Filipino, who's supposed to be handy with a knife?"

Keene laughed and said he had more than one. We took the kid down to the Record room and left him looking at pictures and Keene and I went back to the Homicide room where Linda waited.

I said, "I want to know this, Keene. If the kid picks out the picture of the man he saw by my place, where does it take us? We've got a possible suspect and still no reason for the suspect to do the killing. That don't make anything to give a Grand Jury and expect an indictment."

"We can work on him," Keene said, "and find out what it's all about."

"There's something back of this and I want to know what it

is. I found this dope and you owe me a chance to work on it my own way."

"It's murder. That's police work. I'll pick the bird up, if the kid spots him, and I'll find out everything he knows and it won't take me long. What's your idea, Shean?"

"It's this," I said. "I've got a hunch the guy was after me and just walked into Wilson. He didn't know the difference and Wilson got the benefit. Now I want to know who's after me and why. Do you blame me?"

"Well, no. But this is murder. I can't let it slide."

"I'm not asking you to let it slide. I'm just asking you to give me a little time on it."

"If I find this guy, I'll tell you. We'll go together and pick him up. How's about that?"

I said that was fine, if that was the best he'd do.

Then a uniformed cop brought the kid, Millard Brower, up to us. The kid was all excited and blurted out: "I found him, Mr. Connell. It's the same one, I'm sure. It's a man named Serafino Gomez and he's been in jail already."

Keene started to look restless and I knew he wanted to get at putting out a want for Gomez. I told him where to find the kid, in case he wanted him for identification, and then Linda and the kid and I left.

The boy and I dropped Linda at her house and then I said to him: "We'll go back to your hotel and check you out and then you'll move in with me. I want to keep an eye on you."

"What for?"

"You might be the one who'll put a rope around a killer's neck. Somebody ought to look after you; I doubt if you can look out for yourself."

I got him to promise he'd move in with me the following morning. I dropped him in front of his hotel and noticed the time when I did.

It was just one fifty-five in the morning.

LINDA WOKE ME in the morning. At ten o'clock. I heard her key in the door and when she came in I yanked the covers up around my neck and said, "You shouldn't come in a man's room when he's in bed. It isn't decent."

She was crying a little and she said, "Don't joke, Shean! Look at this."

She held out a paper and I saw "Pinehurst youth slain in hotel" used as a headline. The rest of the story said that Millard Brower, of Pinehurst, had been shot to death in the lobby of his hotel at two-fifteen that morning. Three men had done the job, making sure of it, and none had been identified or recognized as they'd all worn masks. I got on the phone and got Keene and he growled back at me:

"You damn fool! What did you do—spill it around that you had a witness to the real Wilson killer?"

I said, "Now listen. As soon as I found out the kid was a witness, I brought him to you. Ben Levy found the kid for me, but Ben didn't know what I wanted him for and couldn't very well talk about it on that account. I didn't know the kid had seen a thing out of the way until I talked to him, but two of your cops did. Check on them, why don't you?"

"I have. They said the kid hadn't told them a thing about seeing this Gomez there."

I said: "Oke, then. Either somebody was following Linda and me or somebody had been following Kitt and Mahlon.

I dropped him at one fifty-five. That leaves twenty minutes until he was killed. They must have stopped him and talked to him and found out that he'd already been down to the police station."

"Then why would they follow him into the hotel? Why wouldn't they have killed him right where they talked to him?"

"The chances are they had to make up their minds to do the job," I guessed. "He turned and left them and they decided to do him in."

Keene swore and said, "Here's two men killed and no reason for it. It doesn't make sense."

"It doesn't to me either," I said. "I'm not on anything that could give any one reason to kill me. That's what bothers me about it. I'm just on routine stuff that doesn't mean a thing to anybody. Tracing bum checks and that sort of thing."

Keene asked me to come down to the station; I told him I would and hung up.

Linda said, "Mother doesn't know about this yet. I told them at the house to keep the paper away from her. This will just worry her all the more."

"It worries me all the more, hon. Somebody is out after somebody else and I'm afraid it's you and me."

"Why should they, Shean?"

There were answers to this but I didn't give them to her. A private cop makes enemies, in the course of running his business, and that could explain why I was picked for attention.

As far as Linda was concerned, there was her money, which could make trouble. She'd be twenty-one in less than three months and we were planning on being married when she came of age.

I said, "Don't fret about it, hon. As soon as Keene picks up this Gomez, everything will be all right. Keene will find out what it's all about and we'll know what to do."

LINDA HAD TO see her lawyers that morning and I tagged along with her, having nothing better to do. They were in the Graylock Building on First Street. We talked with George Thompson, the partner who took care of Linda's affairs, and Linda gave him the story of what had happened.

Thompson was tall and thin and sour-faced. He looked more like a banker than a lawyer; like the kind of man who enjoyed turning down deserving loans. He pursed his lips, stared up at a corner of the room and said, "This is all very interesting, Miss Wilson. Have you any idea why Augustus Wilson should have wanted to harm Mr. Connell?"

"I can't imagine."

Thompson looked thoughtful. "Let me advance a theory. I understand you and Mr. Connell plan on being married immediately after your birthday. That's in approximately three months."

Linda reached over, got my hand and said, "That's right."

"And I understand you were, well, let us say assisting your step-uncle financially."

Linda said apologetically, "Well, I helped him a little. Things weren't too well with him since the depression."

"Then isn't this theory tenable? Your uncle had the idea that Mr. Connell wouldn't approve of the continued assistance you'd been giving him."

I said, "Sure. But *he* was the man that was killed."

Thompson said softly, "Just a minute, Mr. Connell. I understand Mr. Wilson resembled you to a certain extent. Mr. Wilson wasn't the only relative Miss Wilson has been helping. Maybe the same theory would adjust itself to other people. Think it over."

Linda started sputtering about how her relatives weren't murderers and I started thinking. Linda had about a dozen of her dead stepfather's bum relations on her pension list and, from what I'd heard about some of them, they were a likely lot.

Linda quit arguing about how all her folks were nice people and told him what she was after, which was money. He called in a clerk and told him to make out a voucher for Miss Wilson for a thousand dollars. The clerk looked as though he didn't think much of the idea and said, "But Mr. Thompson…."

Thompson cut him off with: "I know Miss Wilson is a bit behind on her account but that's all right, Griggs. I'll adjust the account later."

He explained to Linda: "You're behind on this quarter's accounts, Miss Wilson. But I can charge this money to my personal account and make the transfer when your dividends come in."

Linda thanked him, took the thousand-dollar check, and we went out. She said, "I've always liked Mr. Thompson. He's looked after things for me ever since my stepfather died. He's been very kind."

"He's got general power of attorney, hasn't he? I mean he can act for you in any way he sees fit, without consulting you."

"Why, of course."

I said I thought that was fine, which I didn't, and spent the next two hours wangling from her the list of the relatives she'd been helping.

The relatives were a fine lot and scattered from here to Halifax. Her own people, that is, the people on her mother's side, were all right. Her stepfather had been a chiseling bum however, and it seemed to run in his family. She'd been helping a bunch of yeggs who would cut a throat for three dollars in cash or five on the cuff. I put Ben Levy looking up the three that lived in town, sent wires tracing the others.

Ben Levy dug up stuff on the three relatives who were in town, and it didn't take him long. Linda's Cousin Bert was in jail. He'd gone in a shoe store, bought one pair of shoes, and started to walk out with two. Uncle Bert Sr., and Cousin Eddy were out, however. Ben said, "The two of them hang down around the bay, rolling drunks."

Linda was giving each one of the three from fifty to a hundred dollars a month, so I asked: "What do they find to do with their dough? Did you find that out?"

Ben laughed. "They're all three horse players. Did you ever see a horse player that had any money?"

I told Ben to keep a tag on the two that were out of jail and to let me know what they did and when they did it.

FOR THREE DAYS things went along with no move. Ben Levy kept calling me and telling me that Linda's Uncle Bert and Cousin Eddy weren't doing a thing they shouldn't. I got wires from agency men in the places the rest of the relations were and, apparently, all the others were tending to their knitting, too.

And then, on Friday, Sergeant Keene came up to my place. He looked sober and sorry and he said, "I've got some bad news, Shean. You know Kitt and Mahlon have been going right along on this business, don't you?"

I said Kitt would work like hell if he thought he had a chance to deal me any misery.

"It's partly that," Keene said. "But I think Kitt honestly thinks you and Miss Wilson are mixed in this. I can't take him off the case because he'd go over my head and claim I was protecting you because of friendship."

"I can see that."

"He thinks Linda killed her uncle. And he thinks you, in turn, killed young Brower. You had no alibi for that time, you know."

"How could I have, the way it came up? I can show I got back to the hotel around two-thirty but the distance from where Brower was killed and where I live can be covered in that fifteen minutes. If it comes to that, Kitt may claim I had the three men spotted there and waiting for the kid when I brought him back. I don't think I can be convicted on the charge, but it'll wreck Linda on the Wilson killing. My testimony won't carry one bit of weight."

Keene nodded and reached for his hat. He said soberly, "The Grand Jury meets on Monday. Kitt and Mahlon and Benny Fox from the D.A.'s office have been together the last two days. My guess is there'll be an indictment returned against you and Miss Linda before Monday evening. Murder against her and probably the same against you. At the very least you'll be held as a material witness. It's a damn shame we haven't been able to pick up Gomez."

I said, "Thanks, Keene. I'll not forget it," and meant it. He was doing more than ninety-nine out of a hundred cops would do in telling me what was coming up on Monday.

Then I called up Linda and she came down that evening, I told her what was coming up. We talked it over and decided the best thing to do was make arrangements with her lawyer before anything happened, so she called him and made an appointment for ten the next morning.

He said, "Of course, Linda, I'll help in any way I possibly can, but my practice hasn't been in the criminal court and I don't feel competent to handle this for you."

She said, "We'll talk about it in the morning," and hung up. I said: "He'll do as good as anybody else. It's going to take money for bail. And pull, to get the case handed over to Raoul LeFevre. LeFevre's the kind of a guy that likes to help people. He'll admit you to bail, where a tough judge wouldn't."

The phoned buzzed then and I picked it up and Ben Levy said, "Here's some news, Shean, if it means anything. Your girl's uncle and cousin just made the can. They were down on Alvarado Street in a crap game. There were four shines and three or four Filipino boys in the game and the uncle and cousin and another white man. There was an argument and one of the gugus came out with a shiv and the battle started. Two of the shines and all of the Filipinos got away, but the cops got Uncle and Cousin, the other white man, and two of the shines. One of the shines is pretty badly cut up and the other white man is slashed a bit."

I said: "Check it, Ben. Find me the names of all of the bunch in it. Tell Uncle and Cousin I'll try and bail them out tomorrow, if I can."

I hung up the phone and said to Linda: "That's another reason you'll have to see your lawyer in the morning. Your uncle and cousin got in the can over a cutting scrape and you'll have to go bail for them. That is, if you want to do it."

She said, "I bet it wasn't their fault. They're not the sort of people who get in trouble, Shean."

"They're right," I told her, "and the cops and the rest of the world are wrong. What I want to know is this: Was Serafino Gomez one of the gugus in this scrape? That would mean a tie-up with your uncle and cousin on the other thing." This started an argument. I stopped it by taking her to dinner. After we ordered I went to the phone booth, got Keene on the line, and said, "Suppose you work over Bert Wilson and Eddy Wilson and see if you can find anything about Serafino Gomez. They're in your jail for being in a cutting affair. This might be the pay-off."

Keene laughed and said, "Give me credit for a little something anyway, Shean. They're in the star chamber right now. I got Jerry on their names when they were brought in and I'm trying to find out who the Filipinos were that ran out of the game. Right this minute. Kitt and Mahlon and a couple of the other boys are working them over."

I went back to the table and Linda asked suspiciously, "Who were you calling?"

"The station, hon. I just called Keene and told him to go easy on your uncle and cousin. That's all."

"I'll bet that's all."

I stuck to my story... and was stuck with it. She spent the four hours between then and the time I took her home wailing about how the world didn't give Uncle and Cousin a break.

Loyalty's a fine thing... but it can be misplaced.

GEORGE THOMPSON, THE lawyer, had his office on

the third floor and we got there fifteen minutes early the next morning. We went inside the reception room and the clerk there looked at us doubtfully and said, "Aren't you a bit early, Miss Wilson? I'm afraid Mr. Thompson is busy right now. I'll tell him you're here."

I reached for a cigarette, but I only had one left in the package. I gave it to Linda and said, "You'll have to wait a minute or so, hon. I'll just run downstairs and get some."

"Well, hurry, Shean."

"I'll just be a minute," I told her, and went out in the hall. I closed the door to the reception room behind me and, just as I did, the door farther up the hall closed and a man hurried past me toward the elevator. He was just average size and build but he wasn't average in color. He had the half-Indian, half-Chinese look that a good many Filipinos have. I followed him down the hall to the elevator and he looked at me and through me, in the way people do when they don't know you and don't want to. The elevator boy nodded at him as though he'd seen him before and the Filipino grunted hello and that it was a nice day. He had no accent, that I noticed. We got out on the street level and I stopped and got cigarettes at the stand there and watched him climb in a cab. It pulled out into traffic and I got the one next in line and said:

"See the hack right in front of us?"

The hacker said, "That's Ted's cab. Sure I see it."

"Swell," I said. "As long as you know it, there's no excuse for you to lose it."

He got the idea—too well. He stepped our hack along until we weren't more than three feet behind the first one and apparently he meant to hang on there. I said, "Listen, bud! If I'd wanted to ride with the guy in front I'd have climbed in with him. Drag back."

"Maybe I'll miss him."

"You dope. If you do, we can find out where he went when the cabbie goes back to the stand. Drop back; I don't want the guy to wise up he's being tagged."

We dropped back and the leading cab swung down toward the docks, went along the water front for a dozen blocks, then turned sharply and headed up a steep hill. It pulled into the curb, halfway up this, and I got money in my hand and said:

"Pull in right behind them. Now when I climb out, tell that friend of yours in the cab ahead to get the hell away from there. And you beat it, too. Get it?"

He said he understood but he didn't sound as though he did and I wanted no mistakes. I handed him the money and explained, "If there's any fuss, I don't want a car handy around there. This guy ahead will be on foot and that's the way I want him to be. Now d'ya see? Give some of this dough to your pal."

He said yes and sounded as though he meant it this time. We made the stop, right behind the other hack. I jumped out and said to the Filipino:

"Hey, there! Just a minute."

My driver was talking to his friend and I heard the gears mesh on the first cab. It started to pull away while the Filipino turned and faced me and said, "Yes! What is it?"

I said, "I want to talk with you," while my cab made a U-turn and followed the first hack down the street.

He said, "I don't know you," and he said it as though he was glad of it.

I said, "You know of me, guy. The name's Connell. Let's go

inside that house you were heading for and have a little talk."

He didn't change the expression of his face one bit. "We can talk here as well as inside. I don't know you. What do you want?"

I got my hand inside my coat and slipped my gun out of the clip that held it. The house we were standing in front of was like the rest of the ramshackle lot around it and it was hemmed in on each side. At least a dozen people were sitting on their porches and not paying any attention to us, but from their looks they were all Filipinos and I didn't want to start any race riot with them, so I kept the gun hidden.

I said, "If you don't know me a talk won't hurt you. But we can go down to the station and talk there, if that's the way you want to make it."

"Why should I go down to the station?"

I didn't answer this, just moved the gun a bit under my coat. He stared at the bulge the gun made, then at me. He said, in the same flat voice: "It's that way, huh?"

He turned and started for the house and I followed him through a littered yard. We went up on a porch that felt as though it might break under our weight and he lifted his hand to knock on the door. I got the gun clear, though still keeping my coat over it, and said:

"Just walk right in. You don't have to signal anybody. They heard the two cabs stop."

He opened the door and went in and I waited until he'd got to the center of the room and followed him. I could see the entire room, could see it was empty, and I said to the Filipino, "Isn't anybody home?"

Then, *wham!* right on my head.

I WOKE UP some time after that. Over in the corner of the room, lying on my back, with my hands tied across my chest with sash cord and my ankles laced together with the same stuff. A little Filipino with a scarred face was squatting on his heels by me. I knew from his picture that Millard had identified that he was Gomez. When he saw me open my eyes he grinned at me and said:

"Hagh! You come in. I wait for you. Behind the door, I wait for you. How you like?"

"I don't like," I said, and moved my head. I thought this was going to kill me. It felt as though it was going to split wide open.

The scarred little man kept his grin and said, "I hit you. Not hard. With a piece of pipe."

"With the same piece of pipe you hit Gus Wilson with?"

He shook his head and said he hadn't hit Gus Wilson with any piece of pipe. The door beyond him opened and a very blond, very hard looking gal came in then. She was only about twenty but she looked as though she'd been everywhere and done everything. She saw I was awake and said, "You dumb shamus! You walked into something, didn't you? And us getting good money to put you out of the way and you walk in and ask for it. It's a laugh."

I wasn't laughing. I asked, "Are you the one who called the station and told them I was dead? After your boyfriend here killed Wilson?"

"He didn't kill Wilson by himself. He didn't do that alone."

The Filipino stood up then and I saw he wasn't much over five feet tall, if any. He didn't look as though he'd weigh more than a hundred pounds if he were wringing wet. He kept his open grin, showing me a lot of gold teeth.

I said, "Who did kill Wilson?"

She didn't answer me but said to the Filipino: "Pedro's gone to the corner to telephone and get some groceries. I'm going to have him get the dough for this job before we do it. You start packing now. We'll go south tonight."

"For why we go south?" the scarred man asked.

She said impatiently, "Don't be a nut. Maybe we should stick around here and take a chance on being picked up? What's the use of having money if we can't get action with it? We'll go out tonight; Pedro'll drive and you'll ride in back under a robe until we're clear of town. Not that they're stopping cars but why take chances?"

I said, "Listen, sister. This bird is Serafino Gomez and the cops are looking for him for murder. They've got his prints, his picture, and his record. He's hotter than a forty-five, right now. The smart thing for you to do would be to turn him in to the cops after you turn me loose from this. That'll clear you and give you an out."

She came over then and kicked me in the face. Not hard but just casually. She said, "Keep your big mouth shut," to me, and to the Filipino: "You heard me. Get at that packing."

He said, "Yes, mama," and left the room.

She stood staring down at me and said, "You're money in our pocket, guy. Big money. And the way I've worked it, there's no chance for a cross in the deal. We're protected all the way through."

"I can see you're a smart kid," I told her. "By the time you've done twenty years I'll bet you'll figure out you're in the can. You slipped plenty, sister. Don't think you haven't."

"How?"

"The guy that hired you to kill that kid in his hotel lobby will turn you in like a shot. You can't prove he hired you and the cops will work on these gugu pals of yours and get the truth. Where'll you be then?"

She said, as if she was explaining things to a child: "He was with Gomez and Pedro when they did it. He's in as deep as they are. He'll play hell turning us in. Besides, the cops won't get any of us."

She put out her foot and rubbed the sole across my face, then turned and followed the little scarred man from the room. I tried to break loose from the rope around my ankles and wrists, found it was useless, and then twisted until I was on my side and looked around. The Filipino hadn't bothered me much, but the blond wench really had me scared. Badly enough to have me sweating all over and to have my stomach shaking. She was so easy and matter-of-fact about the whole thing. If she'd shown the least sign of emotion it wouldn't have taken me that way.

The funny thing is that I kept thinking about Linda waiting for me in Thompson's office and wondering just what kind of a bawling out she was planning on giving me for telling her I'd be right back and then not showing up. I had a notion it would be a beaut and thinking about this kept my mind from worrying about the spot I was in myself.

It was probably because of this that I didn't notice the razor blade right at first. It was flat on the floor; one of the single-edged kind and covered with rust. I could hear the blond girl's mean voice telling the scarred man where to put this and that and I could hear him answer every now and then: "Yes, mama."

I went to work, hoping she'd keep him busy. I rolled over on my face and inched up along the floor, until I got my fingers on the rusty blade. The floor was warped and out of plumb, and I fooled around until I found a crack and managed to wedge the blade in this so it seemed fairly solid. I couldn't be sure; I could arch my body up until I could see the blade all right, but I couldn't tell how it was fastened in the crack. I rolled over on my side again, inched down a bit until I could get the side of my wrists against the edge of it, and started to saw away.

The blade pulled out as soon as I touched it and I had to do the thing over again, and by that time I was so wet with sweat that my fingers were slippery and I had a hell of a time making the blade stay with the edge upright. But it finally did and this time it stayed where I'd put it. Wobbly, but it stayed.

I sawed away for what seemed like an hour. I was cutting my wrist as much as I was the rope around it because, by that time, my arms were tired and I was shaking all over from excitement. But the rope frayed; parted, and I sat up and started to untangle the piece that was around my ankles.

I just got this unfastened when a voice said, "I got back just in time, I see."

I looked up and saw the one called Pedro leaning against the door and smiling at me. He was holding a Luger in his hand, with the muzzle of it bearing on me, and he lifted his voice and called, "Gomez! May! Come here."

The scarred Filipino and the girl came in the room and May said viciously: "This wise ——!"

The scarred one said, in a puzzled voice: "Hagh! I leave him tied. He is untied. How does it?"

Pedro said, "I thought you were going to keep an eye on him?"

May started to swear at me and she knew all the words and used them. Pedro listened to it, grinning and holding the Luger so it centered me. Gomez listened also, but now he looked a little crazy. He was licking his lips with the tip of his tongue and making funny noises in his throat. He stopped the girl by saying in a husky voice: "By ———, I fix him now."

She shut up in the middle of a word. Gomez reached up to the back of his neck and brought out a knife from between his shoulder blades. It was a thin-bladed affair and looked as though it had once been a paring knife. Cheap looking, but I had the notion it would make as ugly a hole in me as an expensive knife would. He started to walk toward me, stooping a little bit, and I waited for him, drawing my knees up under me.

Pedro said suddenly, "Wait! I'll hold him!" He motioned at me with the gun and said, "Stand up!"

I stood up, figuring it was better to take it standing if it were going to happen. And also, that I'd have more of a chance if I was on my feet. He handed the Luger to the girl, saying: "The safety's off. Now watch him."

She said: "I'll watch the ———."

Pedro moved past me and behind me and said, "Put your arms behind you."

I didn't move. He reached down and caught both my wrists and the girl tightened her finger on the trigger and acted as though she wanted an excuse to pull it. I let my arms go back. Pedro pulled them up behind me, in the start of a double hammer-lock, and said to the scarred one: "Now, Gomez! Now!"

Gomez was panting like a dog. He was holding the knife ahead of him, making little short stabbing motions with it, and he edged in at me from the side. The girl took a couple of steps ahead, holding the gun at her side and against her hipbone, and she said to him: "Give it to him, lover."

She turned her head toward him when she said this and I went as high in the air as I could, using the hold Pedro had on my arms as a prop, and kicked her in the stomach with both feet. I could see her head jerk forward as she started to double up and then the recoil from the kick took effect on Pedro and he stumbled backward and let me fall. I'd been bridged in the air and, lashing out with my feet the way I had, shoved him back with a lot of force.

I landed flat on my back and Gomez made a whistling sort of gasp and tried to fall on top of me with the knife. I caught his wrist as he came down with it, got my other forearm under his chin and shoved him away. He was so little this was easy. I kept hold of his wrist and dragged him along the floor with me until I could reach the gun the girl still held, and I got this and turned just in time to see Pedro picking up a chair.

I shot at him then but I wasn't used to the gun and I had to try it three times before I centered him. He dropped the chair and sat down on the floor and I took the gun and swiped the barrel across Gomez' jaw. I hit harder than I intended and I could hear the bone crunch. Then I looked at the girl.

She was lying flat on her face and her face was blue. She was as limp as a rag and breathing as though she had asthma. I said aloud, for no reason at all because she couldn't hear me: "Well, babe, you've got some broken ribs."

Then I stood up and saw that some way in the fracas I'd managed to roll against the knife. My left arm was slashed from the elbow to the wrist, deep. The coat sleeve was hanging loose from my elbow down. I draped it over the arm, so it would soak up most of the bleeding, then went out the door and to the porch. There were about twenty Filipinos standing outside, in the road, and I called out:

"Will one of you people find a policeman for me?"

Some kid, right in the front of the mob, called back: "Find him yourself."

I heard a whistle pipe up, down toward the foot of the hill and said, "To hell with it," and shot the Luger three times into the porch floor. Then I sat down on the steps to wait for the cops. I knew they'd locate me from the sound of the shots and I felt too sick to move for a while. The blond girl had really scared me.

KEENE SAID, WHILE the police surgeon patched up my arm: "Well, I guess it's the pay-off. I'll get the truth from this Serafino Gomez if I have to take him apart." He grinned at the surgeon and added: "Like you'll take his partner apart when you do the post-mortem."

I said, "It isn't the pay-off yet. We might as well get that over with here and now."

He looked curious and asked what I meant. I said, "We'll stop by my hotel and I'll pick up a bellhop. There's a kid there that's a natural born actor and that's what we're going to need."

He shrugged and said, "I think you're a bit wacky from that slice out of your arm but I'll play along. Are you sure you're all right?"

"He's all right," the surgeon said. "But he ought to get off his feet and avoid excitement. He's lost a lot of blood."

I told Keene: "And I've lost a lot of sleep worrying over this crazy business. It doesn't look so crazy now."

We got in the squad car and went to the hotel and I picked up the boy I wanted. And told him what I wanted him to do while we finished the drive. The three of us sailed in past the clerk in George Thompson's office and to his private room, and when we went in the kid lifted his hand and said:

"That's him. That's him, Mr. Connell. That's the guy I saw coming from your room that day."

Thompson sat back of his desk and stared at us. Linda was across from him and she saw my bandaged arm and ran to me and said, "What's happened, Shean? Oh, honey, are you hurt?"

I fended her away and said, "Hold it for a while, hon." And to Thompson: "We've picked up the others. It's all over. How much are you short?"

He didn't hesitate. He said, "About ninety thousand dollars. I should have known I couldn't get away with it."

Keene said, "Not with murder. Murder's tough."

Thompson shrugged and stood up. He said, "Well, I suppose you'll want me to go along with you. There's no reason to postpone this that I can see."

Keene stared and didn't say anything. Neither did I. I'd expected to have to do a lot of proving and him taking it like that was a shock. He walked from behind his desk, and to a hat-rack, stood there, half-turned from us. He stood there with his left hand in his pocket and said, "How did you know?"

I said, "Well, to start with, you—"

Right then Keene gave a sort of muffled shout and dashed past me. He grabbed Thompson's hand away from his face, wrestled with him for a moment and then stepped back. Thompson faced the rest of us and said, "It's all right. I'd made up my mind just what to do and I've done it. I'm sorry, Linda."

He stood there and the color changed in his face and he started to shake. Keene caught him as he slumped and said, "Poison! I tried to stop him but I was too late. I might have known. Thinking the boy saw him leave your room was the clincher. He knew that would tie him in."

I said, "Oh, hell! I should have known the score on the whole thing long before I did. The State would have hung him, anyway."

Linda was white in the face and could hardly say, "Why, Shean?"

"For killing your step-uncle," I said, "and for being with the two Filipinos when they shot Millard Brower in the lobby of his hotel. The Filipinos made him go along with them all the way. They never gave him a chance to turn on them from the time he started this business. He hired them and then couldn't get rid of them. Their blond girl saw to that.

"He was short with your money, hon, and knew that when you married me he'd have to give an accounting. He could stall you for a while but that would bring things to a head. He hired Serafino Gomez and his pal to help out and they laid for me. Serafino went up the fire-escape to my room, climbed in and held up Wilson, thinking Wilson was me. He let Thompson in the front door of my place and Thompson slugged Wilson over the head. Then that blood-crazy Gomez stabbed him to death while he was unconscious. Later they found out they'd killed the wrong man. They were tagging me, hoping for a chance to do me in, when we picked up the Brower kid and took him to the station, and they stopped the kid when I let him out in front of his place and asked him where he'd been.

The darn fool told them and they shot him to keep him from identifying Gomez as the man he'd seen by my place. Gomez had a lot of Wilson's blood over him; he was kind of crazy and couldn't keep away from Wilson after he was bloody."

Linda shuddered and said, "I'm glad it's over with. How did you know that George Thompson was the man behind it? He tried to pass it to my relatives."

I laughed and said, "Uncle Bert and Cousin Eddy got three months apiece for frequenting a gambling house. I forgot to tell you. Two prize packages, hon, but they'd never seen Gomez."

She got red in the face and looked at Keene, who tried to keep from grinning. She said again, trying to get back to the original subject and away from the relatives: "How did you know it was Thompson who did it?"

I said, "Cinch. The blow that knocked out Wilson was delivered by a lefthanded person. The angle it struck across his head proved that. The matches I found had been dropped by a left-handed person, too. Just additional proof. Thompson was left-handed and that settled it. When I spotted that gugu coming out of here, that made it a certainty."

Linda said, wide-eyed: "But I'm lefthanded, too,"

I said, "Yeah, that's what worried me. I was afraid Sergeant Keene, here, would get that left-handed idea the same as I had."

"I had it," Keene said, "but I was keeping quiet about it. I knew Miss Linda wasn't guilty and I didn't want Kitt and Mahlon to have any more than they had to go on. I'll have to admit, they had plenty as it was."

I said, "That big ape of a Kitt. As soon as my arm's all right I'm going to see just what kind of a dent I can make in him."

"You'll do no such thing," Linda said.

Keene grinned, told her, "It don't do any good to talk to him, Miss Linda. He's the kind of damn Irish fool that has to learn for himself. A good big man will whip a good little man every time."

I said, "I suppose I'll find that out. Oh, well, live and learn, and like it."

www.ingramcontent.com/pod-product-compliance
Lightning Source LLC
Chambersburg PA
CBHW030547030726
47495CB00004B/1165